P9-CQZ-231

DISCARD
PORTER COUNTY
LIBRARY SYSTEM

SURVIVING THE
APPLEWHITES

Also by **STEPHANIE S. TOLAN**

APPLEWHITES AT WIT'S END

THE FACE IN THE MIRROR

FLIGHT OF THE RAVEN

A GOOD COURAGE

LISTEN!

ORDINARY MIRACLES

PLAGUE YEAR

SAVE HALLOWEEN!

WELCOME TO THE ARK

WHO'S THERE?

SURVIVING THE APPLEWHITES

STEPHANIE S. TOLAN

HARPER
An Imprint of HarperCollins*Publishers*

Surviving the Applewhites

For information address HarperCollins Children's Books,
a division of HarperCollins Publishers,
195 Broadway, New York, NY 10007.
www.harpercollinschildrens.com

Library of Congress Cataloging-in-Publication Data
Tolan, Stephanie S.
Surviving the Applewhites ; by Stephanie S. Tolan.
p. cm.
Summary: Jake, a budding juvenile delinquent, is sent for home schooling to the arty and eccentric Applewhite family's Creative Academy, where he discovers talents and interests he never knew he had.
ISBN 978-0-06-441044-1
[1. Eccentrics and eccentricities—Fiction. 2. Theater—Fiction. 3. Family life—North Carolina—Fiction. 4. North Carolina—Fiction.] I. Title.
PZ7.T5735 Su 2002 2002001474
[Fic]—dc21 CIP
AC

Typography by Erin Fitzsimmons
❖
Revised edition, 2012
15 16 OPM 30

For Ronald Francis Tolan
The bright, creative, funny,
playful, rock-solid stubborn,
and frequently maddening
patriarch of the Tolan clan.

We love you!

Chapter One

"My name is not Edie. It's E.D. *E* period, *D* period."

"What kind of a name is that?"

The boy slouching against the porch railing had scarlet spiked hair, a silver ring through one dark brown eyebrow, and too many earrings to count. He was dressed entirely in black—black T-shirt, black jeans, black high-top running shoes—and the look in his eyes was pure mean.

"My kind," E. D. Applewhite said. She had no

intention of telling this creep the story of her name. She could tell by looking at him that he'd never heard of Edith Wharton, her mother's favorite writer. Being probably the only almost-thirteen-year-old girl in the whole country named Edith, she had no intention of giving him even that little bit of ammunition to use against her. E.D., she thought, was at least dignified—like a corporate executive, which one day she just might be. "What kind of a name is Jake Semple?"

Two can play at that game, the boy's face said. "Mine."

Not an original bone in his body, E.D. thought. Just a plain ordinary delinquent.

According to her friend Melissa, though, Jake Semple was famous. He had been kicked out of the public schools in the whole state of Rhode Island. Melissa wasn't sure what all he'd done to achieve that particular distinction, but the word around Traybridge was that one thing he did was burn down his old school. He'd come to North Carolina to live with his grandfather Henry Dugan, a neighbor of the Applewhites, and go to Traybridge Middle School.

The plan had not lasted long. No one in living memory had been thrown out of Traybridge Middle School, but Jake Semple had managed to accomplish that feat in three weeks flat. At least the building was still standing. It was only the middle of September, and he had run out of schools that were willing to risk taking him.

Mr. Dugan was inside at that moment discussing with E.D.'s parents, her Aunt Lucille, Uncle Archie, and Grandpa Zedediah the arrangement the two families and Jake's social worker had worked out for continuing Jake's education.

Jake Semple was the first person E.D. had ever met who had a social worker. She thought that was probably only one step away from having a probation officer, which is what Jake's parents would have when they got out of jail. That was *why* Jake had a social worker—because his parents were in jail for growing marijuana in their basement and offering some to an off-duty sheriff's deputy. E.D. didn't know how long they were going to be in jail, but at least a year. She figured criminal tendencies ran in families. The kid had burned down his school just after his parents were arrested.

E.D.'s Aunt Lucille was a poet and had been conducting a workshop at Traybridge Middle School when Jake was kicked out. This whole terrible idea had been hers. She'd told Mr. Dugan about the Creative Academy, which was what E.D.'s father had named the Applewhite home school. Only Aunt Lucille, whose view of life was almost pathologically sunny, would get the idea that after an entire state had admitted it couldn't cope with the kid and after Traybridge Middle School had been defeated in less than a month, the Applewhites should take him in. The Creative Academy didn't even have any trained teachers, let alone guidance counselors and armed security guards. There were a whole bunch of buildings the kid could burn down at Wit's End—the main house, all eight cottages, the goat shed, a toolshed, and the barn.

But somehow Aunt Lucille had convinced everybody else. E.D. had been the only family member to vote against letting Jake Semple join them. She'd begged her grandfather, who usually had more sense than all the rest of the family combined, to put a stop to the idea. "You know how Aunt Lucille can't ever believe a bad thing about anybody!" she'd told him. "Her attitude about people is downright dangerous."

He'd only twiddled with his mustache and said that he rather envied Lucille's rose-colored view of things. "More often than not, I've noticed, it turns out to be true." Then he had declared taking Jake Semple in a noble and socially responsible thing to do. Noble and socially responsible! More like suicidal, E.D. thought. She had thought that even before she'd laid eyes on Jake Semple. Now she was sure of it.

Jake pulled a cigarette out of a pack in his T-shirt pocket.

"Better not light that thing," she said, thinking about lighters and matches and very large fires. "Wit's End is a smoke-free environment."

The boy reached into his pocket and pulled out a yellow plastic lighter. "You can't have a smoke-free environment outdoors," he said.

"We can have it anywhere we want—this is our property, all sixteen acres of it."

Jake looked her square in the eye and lit the cigarette. He took a long drag and blew the smoke directly into her face so that she had to close her eyes and hold her breath to keep from choking on it. Then he said one of Paulie's favorite phrases. No one had managed to break Grandpa's adopted parrot of swearing. E.D. suspected that they wouldn't have any better luck with Jake Semple.

Chapter Two

So far so good, Jake thought. This girl was bugged by cursing and smoking. He had news for her. He intended to do a whole lot of both. He took a long drag on his cigarette and blew the smoke at her again. She turned away and moved down to the other end of the porch steps. *Doesn't bother me, girl—you can bug off completely as far as I'm concerned.*

Jake hadn't been any more than two years old when he found out how certain words affected people. It had surprised him considerably, since his parents used those words at home all the time. He'd learned them the same way he learned all the other words he knew. People didn't make a fuss when his parents used them, but once he'd seen how some adults reacted to those words when he said them, it had become a game. He could still remember the old woman with the mean, pinched-up face who told him to take his sticky fingers off the display case when his mother took him to the bakery to get a cake on his third birthday. He had smiled his best little-boy smile and said just two words. The woman had gone all white and slumped right down to the floor. The image was as clear in his mind now as if it had happened yesterday—the way she'd just disappeared all of a sudden from behind the counter. All the fuss and furor afterward had made a permanent impression on him. Nobody could ever tell Jake Semple words didn't have power.

If the rest of the Applewhites were anything like this girl, he thought, he ought to be able to bug them quite a lot for however long he was going to be stuck with them. He leaned back against the support post behind him and watched the smoke float out from his nostrils. He hated adults making decisions for him and expecting him to just go along with whatever they said. His parents had tried that and given up. But because of that big mistake they'd made with the sheriff's deputy, they'd been carted off to their separate minimum-security prisons and he was stuck with a bunch of strangers who didn't get it that he wasn't going to do what he didn't want to do. He would just have to show them! He intended his time here to be even shorter than his time at Traybridge Middle School.

The smoking part was going to be a problem, though. This was his last pack of cigarettes. It was miles to town, and out here in the North Carolina boonies there was no such thing as a bus. He squinted against the smoke that was blowing back at him now. Maybe, since there were tobacco fields along just about every road, he could tear off a few leaves and learn to roll his own.

He was pretty sure this girl had been told to keep an eye on him while his grandfather was inside, to make sure he didn't set fire to the porch or something. She wasn't much to look at. Not much shape yet. Still as much like a boy as a girl, and the chopped-off hair didn't help much. She was sitting there now with her scabby elbows on her scabby knees, staring off down the driveway. Jake couldn't see the main road from here, the way the drive curved around a row of trees and bushes, but out there was a wooden sign with WIT'S END spelled out on it with bark-covered twigs. Quaint and rustic and weird. Jake had never known anyone who named their house before.

His grandfather said the place had had a name ever

since he was a kid. It had been a farm till it went bust and somebody bought it, built a bunch of scruffy little cabins up against the woods, and turned it into a motor lodge. They'd named it The Bide-A-Wee, added an office wing, and lived in the big two-story house. Then the Applewhites, all artsy types, his grandfather said, had moved down from New York and bought it. The scruffy little cabins were still there, but now the house was part house and part school.

There were four Applewhite kids, but Jake had only met this one so far—this A.B. or C.D. or whatever her name was. Being home schooled, the Applewhites hadn't been at Traybridge Middle School during what he liked to think of as the Jake Semple Reign of Terror. He wondered what the others were like.

Suddenly there was a scream from somewhere off to the right of the house. A brown-and-white German shepherd–sized animal with huge lopsided horns came tearing around the end of the porch and down toward the road. A long piece of white cloth with flowers on it streamed from its mouth and dragged on the ground, almost tangling in its legs as it ran. Right behind it, shouting at the top of her lungs, came a tall, barefoot girl in a black leotard. Jake nearly choked on the smoke he had just inhaled. This one was easy to recognize as a girl! He thought she might be the most gorgeous girl he'd ever seen. She was running at first, her long, wavy auburn hair streaming out behind her, but she started hopping from one foot to the other when she reached the gravel drive. From then on her shouting kept getting interrupted by little yelps of pain.

The animal she was chasing was a goat. A smelly one. As fast as it had galloped by, it had left its odor very clearly on the air. Goat and girl disappeared around the bend in the drive, but the shouting and yelping went on, getting fainter and fainter.

"Cordelia," the girl on the step said. "And Wolfie."

"What's all the fuss?" Jake's grandfather came out of the house, a fat dog—a basset hound—with ears so long it nearly walked on them with every step, waddling at his heels. The Applewhite adults were right behind.

The oldest of them, a wiry old man with white hair and a droopy white mustache, pushed his way through the others and headed straight for the wooden rocking chair in the corner of the porch. On his way he snatched the cigarette out of Jake's hand so fast Jake didn't know what had happened till it was being ground out on the porch floor under the old man's shoe.

"Smoke-free environment," he said, and sat down on the rocker. "Remember that."

Everybody on the porch, including the basset hound, was looking at Jake, and he felt his face starting to heat up. He looked off the way the goat and the girl had gone, whistling under his breath to let them know that he didn't care. Not at all.

The breathtaking girl in the leotard was picking her way back along the driveway, carrying what was left of the flowered material as if she had a dead baby in her arms. It was smudged with red-brown dirt and dotted with burrs.

"I'm going to murder that goat one of these days!" she said.

Lucille Applewhite, the frizzy-haired blond poet whose idea all this was, ran down the porch steps, one hand over her heart. "You might have murdered him already, yelling and chasing him like that. He's probably lying in a heap under a bush somewhere, drawing his last breath."

"No, he's not. I chased him into the barn."

"Come off it, Lucille," the man with the shaggy dark hair and goatee said. According to the description Jake's grandfather had given him, this had to be Randolph Applewhite, the father of the Applewhite children. "That smelly demon is hostility personified. It would take more than a little chasing to get him down."

"That isn't hostility. Wolfbane is suffering from post-traumatic stress." Lucille turned back to the girl in the leotard. "Whatever were you doing in the goat pen?"

Cordelia stamped her foot and yelped again. She

had apparently forgotten she was standing in the gravel. Jake thought she had a particularly musical yelp. "I was not in the goat pen! I was in the meadow. That beastly, smelly, disgusting creature was running loose. Again! He tried to murder me. It was lucky I had a piece of my costume with me to deflect him."

Lucille let out a squeal. "Loose? He was loose? What about Hazel? Where's Hazel?"

Cordelia stormed up the porch steps, pushed her way through the crowd of people, and stepped over the dog, who had flopped down directly in front of the door. "She's halfway to Traybridge for all I know. Ask Destiny!" The screen door banged shut behind her.

"Destiny?" The woman with reading glasses around her neck, who'd been jotting notes on a little notepad, looked up now, as if she was just tuning in. She was famous, Jake knew. He'd even seen her on television once. She wrote best-selling mysteries about a florist who was an amateur detective. She was also the children's mother, but her name wasn't Applewhite; it was Jameson. Sybil Jameson.

"What about Destiny?" she asked now. "He's taking a nap. I sent him to his room half an hour ago, and he *promised* me he would take a nap." She stuck her notepad into the pocket of her oversized shirt and put her pencil behind her ear. "If he's out by himself somewhere, we'd better find him. No telling what he's getting into."

"He'd better not be in the wood shop again. Last time he drilled holes in a footstool I had nearly finished!" The man who said this had a crew cut and was wearing a denim shirt with the sleeves rolled up to show tattoos on both arms. This would be Archie Applewhite, Randolph's brother and Lucille's husband. He and the old man both made wooden furniture.

"Knowing your work, I can't believe it made much difference," Randolph said. "What are a few drill holes more or less?"

"You're just jealous because I have a gallery show coming up and you're out of work—again."

"Stop arguing and help me find Hazel!" Lucille said. "If she gets out on the road, she'll be killed."

Jake hadn't heard a single car go by the whole time he'd been here. Whoever Hazel was, she didn't seem likely to get run down the minute she set foot on the road.

In a matter of moments, Jake found himself alone on the porch with his grandfather, the old man with the mustache, and the dog. The others had gone off in different directions, Lucille and Archie yelling for Hazel, the others yelling for Destiny.

When the voices faded away, it was quiet on the porch, except for the snoring of the dog. The old man stuck out his hand toward Jake. "Zedediah Applewhite, patriarch of the Applewhite clan," he said. "How do you do?"

Jake looked at the wrinkled, spotted, knobbly old hand. He was not about to shake the hand that had snatched one of his last precious cigarettes.

But he didn't have a choice. The old man grabbed his hand and shook it in both of his, nearly crushing Jake's fingers in an amazingly powerful grip. "Welcome to Wit's End—Furniture Factory, Gallery, Studio, Goat Compound, and Creative Academy," Zedediah Applewhite said.

When the old man let go, Jake shook his hand to make sure the blood could still get to the tips of his fingers. Then he said a few of his favorite words, just loud enough to be sure they were heard.

Zedediah Applewhite didn't so much as blink. "You ought to spend a little time with Cordelia," he said. "She's taught my parrot the French for that. Spanish, Italian, and German, too."

Chapter Three

E.D. sat in the kitchen pushing a mini-wheat around in the milk at the bottom of her bowl, trying to let the shaft of early sunlight that fell across the table cheer her up. She wasn't crazy about mini-wheats, but it was the only kind of cereal left in the house. She'd put her favorite kind on the list, but it was her father's turn to do the grocery shopping, and he'd forgotten. Again.

A dry leaf detached itself from the dying wildflower arrangement in the middle of the table and drifted into her bowl. She fished it out. Cordelia had just gone through a flower-arranging phase, and of course her arrangements had been beautiful. She was a true Applewhite, after all, which meant that whatever creative activity she put her mind to, she did it really well. But she'd gotten bored with flower arranging, and now the bouquets were blackening all over the house. By the time anybody did anything with them, there'd be nothing left but dry, empty stems and slimy water. By then even Cordelia probably wouldn't remember how they'd gotten there. There was a disturbing lack of focus and follow-up in her family.

E.D. didn't know how she could have been born an Applewhite. She wasn't anything at all like the rest of them. Even her mother and Aunt Lucille, who were only Applewhites by marriage, were more like them than she was. Applewhites were enormously talented. She was not. Applewhites thrived on chaos. E.D. wanted organization and sense. Applewhites loved spontaneity. E.D. wanted a schedule and a plan she could count on. Applewhites craved freedom. E.D. wanted structure.

It was way too early for her to be up, but she'd wakened before dawn from nightmares she couldn't quite remember, except that Jake Semple had been in them. She hadn't been able to get back to sleep. This was the day he would be moving in.

The Applewhites were determined to find the good

kid under the bad exterior. It didn't seem to occur to them that the kid might be bad all the way through. His own grandfather, a man who looked a little shell-shocked, seemed all too eager to get rid of him. Hadn't anyone noticed that? E.D. spooned the last mini-wheat into her mouth, put the bowl on the floor for Winston, who was sleeping noisily at her feet, and then sat, elbows on the table, chin resting on her fists, staring into the early sunlight.

Yesterday, after the goats had been rounded up and her four-year-old brother, Destiny, had been found digging for pirate treasure between the circle of carrots and the circle of tomatoes in Lucille's vegetable garden, there had been a family meeting. Everybody had been there except, of course, her older brother, Hal.

Hal was not just a typical introverted artist. Sometime in the last year he had become an actual recluse. He didn't come out of his room except, as far as anyone could tell, in the middle of the night, when he was reasonably certain everyone else would be asleep.

The point of the family meeting had been to outline The Plan for Jake's assimilation into the Creative Academy. It was worse than she'd feared. He was going to be in *her class*.

This ought to have been an impossibility. The Creative Academy did not have classes. One of the main reasons the Creative Academy had been started in the first place was to avoid what her father called "clumping." Applewhites, he said, shouldn't be required to do what other people did just because other people did it—Applewhites weren't like other people.

It had all started when Cordelia was in the seventh grade at Traybridge Middle School and was told by a teacher that she wasn't allowed to paint a zebra black and purple, because zebras were really black and white. The fact that the zebra in question was part of a science report, not an art project, hadn't made any difference to Randolph Applewhite. "*Real* science demands creativity and individuality," he had told the principal when he withdrew his three older kids from the school district the very next day. "Without creativity and individuality, there would be no scientific discovery. No Galileo, no Newton, no Einstein."

If her father had been safely off directing a play somewhere when the zebra issue came up, she and Cordelia and even Hal might still be going to school in Traybridge, to a regular school with schedules and organization and a great many normal people. Including Melissa, her best friend, whom she never got to see in person anymore.

But Randolph hadn't been off directing. He had been at home with time on his hands. Worse, a theater company that had hired him to direct a play for them had called only that morning, to tell him they had decided not to do that play, so they didn't need him after all. He had been feeling rejected. Artists were tricky enough to handle when their work was going extremely well. Rejected artists could be downright dangerous.

Within a week the Creative Academy had been registered with the state department of education and was up and running. It had turned out to be quite easy to start a home school in North Carolina. All that was required was a guarantee that the teachers had high school diplomas. That was no problem. The academy teachers were the Applewhite adults, and all of them except Uncle Archie had finished college. Even Uncle Archie, who had dropped out of high school to travel the world on a tramp steamer, had eventually gotten a G.E.D. so that he could enroll in art school for a while.

It hadn't been necessary to file a curriculum with the state, which was a good thing, because the Applewhites didn't believe in telling the children what to study and when. The Creative Academy wasn't so much a home school as an *un*school. Its students were supposed to follow their own interests and create their own educational plans. Separately. Individually. Creatively. That meant that, except for E.D., nobody had any sort of educational plan at all. And, of course, nobody was ever doing the same thing as anybody else at the same time.

Until now. Now Jake was to follow E.D.'s plan. She didn't want him to. She had created her plan just for her. She had thought it up for herself and she wanted to *accomplish* it by herself. She might not have talent, she might not have a creative bone in her body, but she wasn't half bad at learning. She had reminded the family about the academy's philosophy. About individuality. The case against clumping. But she could have saved her breath. She and Jake Semple were to be a class.

Part of the reason was math. Up till yesterday, she'd liked math.

Nobody else in the family did. Two and two added up to four no matter who added them, and they went right on adding up to four month after month and year after year. It's what E.D. had always liked about it. Everybody else found it boring. If home schooled kids didn't have to take standardized tests once a year—tests that included math—E.D. felt sure there wouldn't be any math learned at the academy at all. Since they did have to take those tests, they took math online. E.D. was exactly where Jake Semple's last report card from the school he'd burned down said he was. Seventh grade. Geometric problem solving. Comparing percentiles and fractions.

E.D. pulled another dry leaf from the dying bouquet. She had told them that she was willing to be clumped with Jake for math—just not everything else.

But it hadn't done any good. Jake Semple needed to do "cooperative learning" so he could become better socialized, they said, and she was the only genuinely cooperative member of the family. Besides, he wasn't the sort of person—yet—who could be expected to come up with his own structure and organization. "He needs to begin, at least, with yours," Zedediah had said. And that had been that.

E.D. thought of the fat three-ring binder that held her curriculum for the first half of this year. It gave her life order. Stability. Predictability. It had taken her a whole week in August to plan it out. There were sections for each subject, and for each one she had written down her goals and listed every project she planned to do to meet those goals. Then she'd made charts and time lines with squares to check off each step as it was completed. So far, she was right on schedule. If she had to catch Jake Semple up on what she had done in each subject so far, it would throw everything into chaos.

Winston was awake now, lying with his stubby front paws on each side of the cereal bowl, lapping up milk and leaking foamy saliva on E.D.'s sneakers and his own ears. E.D. sighed. She loathed and despised chaos.

Chapter Four

When Jake and his grandfather drove in that morning, Lucille Applewhite, wearing capri pants and a billowy blue-and-green flowered shirt, her hair clamped on top of her head and spilling curls in every direction, hurried from the end cottage to greet them. She stood by the truck and burbled on and on to his grandfather about how glad they were to have Jake joining them and how sure she was that they could provide him with just the environment he needed. Jake climbed down from the truck scowling his most ferocious scowl, but she only smiled. Even his silver-spiked black leather collar and his Vampire Zombies from the Beyond T-shirt with the skull and fangs that dripped bright red blood didn't faze her. After a while, when she didn't seem to be running down, his grandfather said he'd better be going, told Jake to behave himself, and drove hurriedly away, spitting gravel and leaving Jake standing next to the duffel bag that held everything he'd brought from Rhode Island with him.

This grandfather he'd only met a few weeks ago couldn't wait to be rid of him, Jake thought. The old man was no match for the likes of Jake Semple.

"Let's get you settled in your room," Lucille said. "And then I'll give you the grand tour."

Jake picked up his bag, but she didn't move. She just stood looking at him, her hands on her hips, her head to one side. Jake intensified his scowl. The combination of this particular expression and this T-shirt, even without the spiked leather collar, had totally unnerved the principal at Traybridge Middle School.

Lucille sighed a long, appreciative sigh. "A radiant light being, that's what you are. A radiant light being!"

Jake very nearly dropped his duffel bag. *Radiant light being!*

"And don't ever let anyone tell you different."

There were plenty of people who'd be happy to tell him different, he thought. He tried to imagine his social worker back in Rhode Island calling him a radiant light being. She had never called him anything, he thought. Not even his name. Mostly whenever she had to deal with him she just sighed a lot and shook her head. This poet woman must be seriously crazy. The sooner he got out of here, the better.

She turned and started back toward the end cottage. "You'll be bunking with Archie and me in our extra bedroom. I hope you won't mind how small your room is. Think of it as cozy. I really think it'll be perfect for you. It was my meditation room till we found out you were joining us. I called it my zen cave. We brought in a bed and a dresser, of course, and it's all been . . ." Jake had no idea what her next words meant. *Fung schwayed,* it sounded like. "So the energy flow is excellent. You'll find it wonderfully centering."

The cottage, like all the others spaced out in a semicircle to the left of the big house, was a silvery gray structure backed up against the woods. Its narrow porch was covered with vines, some of them so thick and powerful looking that they seemed to be in the process of pulling it down altogether. "We call this Wisteria Cottage. You can see why. It's breathtaking in April when the wisteria's in bloom."

Inside she led him into a small living room lined with bookshelves. In the middle of one shelf was a large, framed photo of a man with a round, smiling dark face, black hair, and piercing black eyes. An entire row of small, flickering candles in glass containers surrounded the photo, and a sprig of what looked like goldenrod stood in a narrow vase next to it. "My guru," she said. "Govindaswami. A genuine old soul. You're lucky. He's coming for a visit, so you're going to get to meet him in person. You'll love him. Everybody does."

Across the room to Jake's left, forming a divider between the living room and a small kitchen area, was a couch covered with a red-and-orange flowered throw. Where a coffee table might have been, there was a large, dark, highly polished, rounded wooden object that reminded Jake of a short, fat, shiny hippopotamus. He had never seen anything like it before.

"Ah!" she said as he stopped to stare at the object. "Beautiful, isn't it? It's my favorite of Archie's coffee tables. We're going to lose it for a while, though. He has a gallery show coming up next month, and they especially wanted this one to be in it."

"Coffee table?"

"Well, you couldn't put a cup of coffee on it, of course, but then who would want to? It's wonderfully soul filling, don't you think? That's what all of Archie's furniture is meant to be." Lucille went through an arch into a narrow hall with two doors on one side and one on the other. She flung open the second of the two doors and stepped back. "All yours," she said.

Jake started into the room and stopped. It wasn't

just very, very small. It was also lavender. Walls, ceiling, even the oval braided rug were all a faintly nauseating shade of lavender. The single window was framed with lavender-and-white striped curtains, and the bed was covered with the same material. There was a strong smell in the room that reminded him suddenly of a great-great-aunt who'd come to visit his mother once. Jake rubbed his nose to keep himself from sneezing.

Lucille sniffed appreciatively and pointed to a bowl full of what looked like crushed, dead, gray weeds on top of the dresser, which was the only thing other than the twin bed that would fit in the room. "Dried lavender. Isn't the aroma wonderful? Calming. Centering. Just like the color. After all you've been through, this space should help you begin to breathe again. Think of it as your personal refuge."

Jake dropped his bag onto the bed. Begin to breathe? Not until he'd opened a window and gotten rid of that stinking bowl of dead weeds!

The other door on his side of the hall was the bathroom that the three of them would share, she told him, and the room across the hall was her and Archie's bedroom. "Now! You want to unpack and get yourself settled, or would you like to go over to the house and check out the schoolroom?"

"Schoolroom," Jake said, rubbing his nose again.

The schoolroom was the wing that had been added on to the side of the house to be the office for the old motor lodge, Lucille told him. It looked pretty much like a schoolroom, except that there was no teacher's desk and no blackboards. There were bookshelves spilling over with books, and there were four school desks, the kind with the top that lifted up and the seat attached. Three of them were piled high with papers and books; the other was empty except for a mug holding pens and pencils. The walls were covered with cork, to which papers were pinned several layers deep. There were hand-drawn maps, poems, and stories written on lined paper, drawings in crayon or paint or colored markers, and lots and lots of finger paintings full of unidentifiable shapes in intense rainbow colors. A huge chart labeled THE BUTTERFLY PROJECT hung at the front of the room. Photographs of butterflies were taped to it, and next to each photograph was a printed paragraph.

All the way across one wall was a banner that read EDUCATION IS AN ADVENTUROUS QUEST FOR THE MEANING OF LIFE, INVOLVING AN ABILITY TO THINK THINGS THROUGH. —Z. APPLEWHITE. Jake didn't think anyone in any school he'd ever been to would have agreed with that definition.

Here and there around the room were vases full of dying wildflowers. Along one wall an old door, complete with doorknob, lay across two bright red filing cabinets to form a long desk. On it, almost lost in a litter of notebooks, file folders, computer disks, CDs, and bits of scribbled-on paper, were a computer, printer, and scanner. "Hal has his own computer in his room, so you'll only have to share this with the other three. E.D. made a sign-up sheet for computer time," Lucille said. "It's around here somewhere."

The sound of a chain saw started up outside. "That'll be Archie. He's a lark—early to bed, early to rise." Lucille checked her watch. "Oh, dear. Randolph is bound to yell. He's an owl, you know. Hates to wake up before ten."

Lucille began clearing things off one of the desks now. "This will be yours. Hal never uses it anyway! I'll see what supplies I can find for you. E.D. will tell you later what she's working on. You and she will be a class."

Jake sighed. If he had to be paired with someone for however long he was going to be here, he'd rather it was Cordelia.

Hammering began somewhere above, followed shortly by heavy pounding that sounded like fists on a door. A voice roared down, "Stop that infernal noise! First Archie, now you. Is everybody mad around here? It's the cracking of the dawn!" A child's voice began singing "Pop Goes the Weasel," loudly and slightly off-key.

"Sounds like everybody's up," Lucille said.

Heavy footsteps came down the stairs, followed in

a few moments by others. Voices came from the kitchen, along with considerable clattering and banging of dishes. The hammering, which had stopped briefly, began again. "Pop Goes the Weasel" gave way to "Hickory Dickory Dock." Jake leaned against a bookshelf full of encyclopedia volumes stacked in random order and watched Lucille dig through the mess on the computer desk. Now and again she came up with a legal pad or a spiral notebook or a stick pen. She put these on his desk. After a while the smells of coffee and bacon drifted into the schoolroom, and Jake's mouth began to water.

"Have you had breakfast?"

Jake shook his head. He hadn't felt much like eating at his grandfather's.

"Can't promise what it is—nobody got groceries this week. But whatever, you're welcome to have some. We want you to make yourself at home."

Lucille led Jake to the kitchen. Randolph was standing at the stove, frowning ferociously and poking at a pan of frying bacon with a long fork, a steaming coffee mug in his other hand. He glowered at them as they came in. A towheaded boy who looked about four years old was sitting on a tall stool at the counter, singing about an itsy-bitsy spider at the top of his lungs. The moment he saw Jake, he stopped singing and stared, his mouth open, his blue eyes wide and round.

"Destiny," Lucille said. "The youngest Applewhite."

At the kitchen table behind another vase of dying flowers sat Sybil Jameson, wearing a tattered robe and jotting notes on a yellow pad with a thoroughly chewed pencil. There was a bowl of soggy cereal in front of her. She looked over her reading glasses and nodded somewhat vaguely at Jake before going back to what she was doing.

A voice that Jake recognized instantly came from behind the open refrigerator door. "Where's the cantaloupe? I distinctly remember there was one last piece of cantaloupe in here last night!" Cordelia emerged from behind the door, dressed in a purple leotard, her hair in a long braid down her back. Jake caught his breath. Even first thing in the morning she was beautiful. "Mother! Hal's been stealing food in the middle of the night again." There was no answer. *"Mother!"*

Sybil Jameson looked up. "What did you say, dear?"

"I said, Hal's been stealing food in the middle of the night."

"I wouldn't call it stealing. He has as much right to eat as the rest of us."

"If he wants to eat, he can come to meals with the rest of us. I had my mouth all set for cantaloupe!"

Her mother didn't answer. She was writing again.

"Our new student's here," Lucille said.

Cordelia nodded at Jake. "Hi." Then she turned back to her mother. "I wish you'd go up and talk to

Hal! My morning's completely ruined. I wanted cantaloupe!"

"Bacon's ready," Randolph said, fishing a piece out of the pan and waving it in her direction. "I found a whole package. You can have bacon. And pumpernickel toast."

"Oh, right! And then everybody can start calling me thunder thighs." Cordelia took a container out of the refrigerator and poured herself a glass of thick, disgusting-looking green liquid. "I'll be out in the dance studio. My whole afternoon was ruined yesterday, so I'd appreciate it if everyone would stay away and let me work." She tapped the little boy on the shoulder. He was still staring, silent and goggle-eyed, at Jake. "That means you, Destiny—and the 'poor little goatses,' too!"

Then she was gone, the glass of green gunk in hand, and Lucille was offering Jake a seat at the kitchen table. The little boy stared at him intensely as he sat, then climbed down from his stool and came to stand at Jake's elbow.

"How did your hair get that color?" he asked. Even if Jake had intended to reply, he couldn't have. The boy went right on, leaving no time for Jake to squeeze in so much as a syllable. "Did it just grow that way? *Mine* just growed. My hair's blond. Did you know they don't gots a blond crayon even in the sixty-four box? I think they should, don't you? Lots of people gots blond hair. What do you call your color? I bet they gots a crayon for *it*. I like it! And how do you make your hair all stick up in points like that? When I wake up in the morning, mine sticks up sometimes. But not in points. Mommy always combs it down. Can you comb your points down?" The boy took a breath and kept going. "Does it hurt to have that ring sticking through your eyebrow? It looks like it hurts. How come you gots so many earrings? What does your shirt say? Is that a pirate skull? It doesn't have the crossbones like a pirate flag. I like pirates. I wanna be a pirate when I grow up. And a painter. And a king. If you—"

Lucille put a plate of bacon and toast in front of Jake. "Don't mind Destiny. He can go on like that all day."

"It's better not to get him started," Randolph said, as if it had been Jake's fault. *"And will you stop that infernal hammering!"* he bellowed up at the ceiling.

Chapter Five

When she finished her breakfast, E.D. had gone out to the meadow with her butterfly net and camera. Winston had lumbered along with her. She was hoping to finish the collecting part of her butterfly project. It was the project she most hated to think of sharing with Jake Semple. First of all, she wouldn't trust a kid like that with anything as beautiful and fragile as a butterfly. Second, it was her favorite project, and she was very, very nearly finished.

The project plan was to catch, photograph, and

catalog every butterfly in the book *Butterflies of the Carolinas*. She'd started in August and gone out every single day, starting in the meadow where there were usually at least a few, and then covering every square inch of Wit's End. She'd found every one of them, from the tiny gray hairstreak to the big eastern tiger swallowtail, except one. If she could find that last one—the great spangled fritillary—now, today, she could close out the main part of the project and keep from having to let Jake loose on the world with a butterfly net.

She'd been out for two hours now, and the sun was getting hot. Sweat was dripping into her eyes and running down her back under her T-shirt. She'd been around the property once and was back in the meadow. No great spangled fritillaries. The only butterflies she had found were the ordinary little cabbage whites and sulphurs she had already caught millions of times. And two red-spotted purples. She couldn't understand it. If she could find both the monarch *and* the viceroy, which looked almost exactly alike, and get photographs that showed how to tell them apart, why couldn't she find a fritillary? Winston, his short legs and his chest all muddy from wading into the pond for a drink, was flopped in the shade of the honeysuckle by the fence. She was beginning to feel like flopping with him.

"E.D.! Wait for us." Lucille was waving at her from the other side of the meadow. "We're doing the grand tour."

Jake Semple was with her, his scarlet hair flaming in the sun. E.D. sighed. Maybe she could just not mention the butterfly project. Maybe she could say she was studying the life cycle of slugs for natural history.

As Lucille and Jake tramped through the woods, crossed the creek, and skirted the pond, E.D. trailed behind them, with Winston trailing behind her. All the while, she kept her eyes peeled for a great spangled fritillary.

At Lucille's vegetable garden, Winston flopped in the shade again while Lucille explained to Jake that nature spirits had told her to make the garden round instead of rectangular and that they came into her dreams sometimes to give her advice about planting and cultivating. Jake rolled his eyes several times during her explanation, and even groaned once or twice. E.D. was so used to her aunt's weird notions that she'd forgotten how strangers tended to react. Jake was being disgustingly rude, but Lucille didn't seem to notice.

At the goat pen Lucille made E.D. tell the story of the rescue of Wolfbane and Hazel because she said she got too choked up to tell it herself. As E.D. explained how the goats, abused, abandoned, and starving, had turned up in the Applewhites' woods in the middle of the winter, Lucille's eyes brimmed with tears. Jake, unmoved, leaned on the fence, his nose wrinkled against Wolfie's ever-pungent odor. E.D. had read somewhere that future serial killers began by abusing animals. She made a mental note to alert someone if he started hanging around the goat pen.

When Wolfie got that crazed look he sometimes got in his eyes and charged the fence, smacking into the fence post right where he was standing, Jake barely flinched. The kid was not normal, E.D. thought. Grown men had been known to flee in terror from Wolfie when he got that look. Just a week ago one of Hal's UPS deliveries had been dumped on the driveway instead of brought up to the house because Wolfie had gotten out of the pen and terrorized the driver.

On the way to show Jake the wood shop, they passed Zedediah's cottage, where Paulie stood on his t-perch in the shade of the narrow front porch. The parrot looked up from picking at one foot with his beak, raised his green, yellow, and red wings, and swore a long stream of colorful curses. Jake swore back. "Don't encourage him," E.D. said. Jake swore some more. Two of a kind, E.D. thought. Birdbrains, both of them.

In the wood shop Zedediah and Archie were both at work, Zedediah at the lathe turning spindles for one of his trademark rocking chairs and Archie carving a series of complicated lines and squiggles into the legs of a turtle-shaped object. "End table," Archie said when E.D. asked. "One of the pieces for the gallery show."

Zedediah turned off the lathe and took off his

safety glasses. "Lucille get you set up with a desk in the schoolroom yet?" he asked Jake.

Jake nodded.

"Good. Don't think that just because there isn't a teacher standing over you every minute, we don't take education seriously. The most important thing you're going to learn while you're here is who you are and what you're made of." E.D. thought they were all likely to learn that about Jake. She was quite sure she didn't want to know.

When they got to the cottage that was the dance and music studio, they didn't go in. The strange, cacophonous music Cordelia had written and recorded for her ballet was blaring from inside. Lucille told Jake just to peek in the window so he could see the studio without disturbing Cordelia while she was rehearsing. He stood there with his nose pressed to the window glass a lot longer than he needed to just to see the floor-to-ceiling mirrors they'd put in, E.D. thought.

When they'd finished the tour, without E.D. seeing even a single butterfly, much less a fritillary, they went back to the schoolroom, where Winston collapsed under the computer desk and began, almost immediately, to snore. It occurred to E.D. that the dog didn't get enough exercise.

"Why don't you show Jake your curriculum notebook?" Lucille said. "He can see what interests him most and get started. I'm going to get rid of these poor bouquets. They're pulling down the energy of the whole room."

E.D. wished she'd written up some bogus projects to send Jake off in completely different directions from her own—something like the history of the pickle industry, or the place of the preposition in English grammar. But it was too late. She got out her notebook and opened it on the top of what used to be Hal's desk. Jake was leaning against the computer desk, his arms folded across his chest.

"Aren't you going to look at it?"

"Why should I?"

"Well, duh! This is a school. We're a class. And this is what we're doing." It occurred to E.D. that she was sounding as if she was in favor of this whole idea. "Suit yourself," she said. She got out the Civil War novel she had started, settled at her desk, and pretended to read.

He began wandering around the room, picking things up and putting them down again. "Where's your TV?" he asked after a while. She pretended to be too engrossed in her reading to hear. "I *said* where's your TV?"

She sighed. "There's one in Zedediah's cottage."

Jake swore. "You mean there isn't one anywhere else in this whole place?"

"We don't watch much television," E.D. said. Sometimes, especially when her friend Melissa was talking about the cable channels she watched all the time, E.D. wished they were like a normal family, with cable and a TV set in almost every room. But just at this moment, she was glad they weren't. "We have better things to do with our time."

Jake swore again. E.D. made an effort to focus on her book.

After a while she heard Jake slump into the seat at his desk. "I don't see any math in here. Don't you do math?"

She looked up. He had actually opened her curriculum notebook. "We do math online. You've already been signed up for the same course I'm doing, with the same tutor."

"Could've saved themselves the trouble," he said.

E.D. ignored him and went on reading. She'd actually managed to get engrossed in the story.

By the time Lucille had come back from disposing of the wildflowers, Jake had turned on the computer. "No games!" he said when she came in.

She smiled. "No games." She clicked off the power on the power strip the computer was plugged into. "And no using the computer without signing up first." Jake swore. Lucille took no notice. "Now then, you've seen the curriculum—what would you like to start with?"

Jake shrugged. "Who says I want to start?"

Lucille clapped a hand over her mouth. "How

thoughtless of me. Giving you an open-ended choice like that on your first day. It's bound to take you a little time to get used to the way we do things." She looked around the room, and her eyes lit on the Butterfly Project chart. "Butterflies!" she said. "Perfect! There's an empty space on E.D.'s chart that needs filling. How about the two of you go out and see if you can find a—what is it?" She peered more closely at the chart. "A great spangled fritillary. That'll get you back outdoors and it won't seem so much like schoolwork."

E.D. groaned. If Lucille was going to start deciding what they were supposed to work on when, why couldn't she decide they should start with the Civil War or *A Midsummer Night's Dream*?

"Get the net out again," Lucille told E.D. She turned back to Jake. "You'll settle in in no time. You'll see. Human beings are almost infinitely adaptable. This is all going to work out brilliantly!"

A few minutes later E.D. and Jake were headed back out to the meadow with Winston tagging after them, huffing noisily as he waddled along. E.D. kept hold of the net. She caught a fiery skipper to show him, explaining carefully that she didn't kill them and mount them, she only photographed them and let them go again. "This is one I already have," she said as she opened the net and let it fly away. "You can read about them all in the book." As she spoke, a black swallowtail fluttered over the honeysuckle and into the meadow, the sun catching the spots of yellow against its black wings.

Jake snatched the net from her hand and went after it. He swept the net and missed, swept again, and the butterfly wavered up and over the fence, then disappeared into the branches of a sweet gum tree on the other side. Jake swore. "Stupid thing to do, catching butterflies."

"So don't! You can do something else for natural history."

"Yeah, well, I don't intend to be here long anyway." Jake swung the net lightly across the tops of the grass and weeds, sending puffs of thistledown into the air.

Good, E.D. thought. "Where do you intend to go?"

Jake shrugged and swept the butterfly net at a dragonfly that veered sharply, changed course, and sped away. "Back to Rhode Island."

"Yeah? Dad says your social worker told him there aren't any more foster families there who'll take you. If you go back, they're going to send you to Juvenile Hall. They must have some kind of school there. You'd probably like it better than this one. At least the other students would be more your type."

Jake didn't say anything. He just struck at the tall grass as if the net were a scythe—one way, then the other—scattering seed heads and blossoms of Queen Anne's lace.

Chapter Six

Jake sat on the front porch steps of the main house, earphones in his ears, his Walkman radio clipped to his belt, picking at a bit of loose rubber on the sole of his shoe. He hadn't been able to find the sort of station he wanted, so he'd had to settle for Top One Hundred hits. It was the first time he'd been alone all day. E.D. had gone off somewhere, and Lucille had told him he could do whatever he wanted till dinner.

She hadn't said when dinner would be. Or what. He wondered what sort of food they served where his parents were. Better, he bet! It was just possible, if the meals here were anything like lunch—Archie had fixed tofu burgers that Jake had found so completely inedible he'd fed his in bits to the fat old basset hound under the table—that the question of whether he would stay or not would be irrelevant. He'd starve to death.

He kept replaying in his mind what E.D. had said out there in that field full of weeds and bugs. That if he didn't stay here there was no place to go except Juvenile Hall. That's what his social worker had told him when she called to talk to him about the Creative Academy. "This is your last chance," she'd said. But people had been saying stuff like that to him all his life. They hadn't really meant it. Did they this time? Did he dare take the chance?

It had been easy to blow off Traybridge Middle School. Everybody—kids, teachers, even the principal—had been scared of the bad kid from the city. *Bad kid.* Living up to that label was what Jake did best. All during the Jake Semple Reign of Terror, he hadn't really thought about what would happen next. Now he knew. This was what. Wit's End and the Applewhites. But what about after this? Would they really send him to Juvie?

"The other students would be more your type," E.D. had said. He thought about the guys at home who'd gone to Juvie. The druggies and the ones who bragged about the guns they could bring to school if they wanted to. It was one thing to be *thought of* as the bad kid from the city. It was something else again to be locked up with real ones.

The dog was sitting a few feet away from him, staring at him with mournful, heavy-lidded eyes. Every so often it made a low sort of moaning sound he could hear over the music in his ears. "What do you want?" he asked. "I don't have any more tofu burger, if that's what you're after." The dog was as crazy as the rest of them, he thought. No normal carnivore would have gulped down tofu burger the way this one had.

"No food, see? Nothing." He held up his empty hands toward it. "Go away!" But it didn't go. It sighed a long, shuddery sigh and sank to the floor, its chin on its outstretched front paws, still staring at him. It was impossible to ignore the expression on its face—as if it had lost its last friend in the world. Jake patted the dog gingerly on the head. It licked his hand. He rubbed it a little behind one ear, and it flopped to its side and then rolled on its back, its stubby little legs in the air. He scratched its chest and it made such a satisfied sound that Jake had to laugh. It closed its eyes then, and after a moment was snoring peacefully, its legs twitching now and again.

Jake's stomach rumbled as he thought over his alternatives. He thought of the banner in the schoolroom—"the ability to think things through." Applewhites or Juvie. Applewhites or Juvie. It wasn't hard to think things through this time. The choice was clear. One way or another, he was going to have to make this work.

A car went by out on the road, and Jake looked at his watch. A little after five. This must be what passes for rush hour in the boonies. He sighed. There wasn't anything to do here. He wasn't about to go to the old man's cottage and ask to watch TV. He'd gone to the schoolroom to do a little web surfing, but Cordelia had been doing her math on the computer. He'd hung around for a while, looking in the book about butterflies to see what kind he'd missed catching in the meadow, just to be near her, but she was so focused on what she was doing that she didn't even seem to know he was there. And he certainly didn't feel like going back to his lavender room.

Suddenly, a white-blond head popped up out of the bushes to his right. Jake was so startled that he jumped and woke the dog, who barked once before turning over and sinking back to sleep. Big round blue eyes gazed at him with fierce intensity.

He pushed back his earphones. "What do *you* want?" he asked Destiny.

The little boy whispered something he couldn't hear.

"What?"

Destiny looked around, like a spy scanning for witnesses, and then scrambled up and sat next to Jake, leaning against him to whisper in his ear. "Did you use matches?" He made a gesture like striking a match. "I'm not allowed to have 'em. Not ever. They say I'm too little. Am I too little, you think? I don't think so. I'd be careful. I used to be little." He held his hand an inch from the porch floor, as if to show a tiny person. "When I was this big, I couldn't have matches. But I could have 'em now, don't you think? Don't you think?" the boy asked again. "You're not that much bigger 'n me, are you? How old are you?"

This time he stopped long enough for Jake to answer. "Fifteen."

"Are not. I know 'cuz Grandpa said you're the same as E.D. That means you're only twelve."

"I'm thirteen," Jake said. Destiny looked doubtful. "I am!"

"Well?" Destiny said. "Did you use matches?"

Jake told him he didn't know what he was talking about. It wasn't until Destiny yelped that he realized he'd used the F word.

"Momma says only Paulie's allowed to say that word. It's not a people word; it's a parrot word. Paulie knows lots of parrot words."

"It is too a people word," Jake said.

"Is not!"

"Is too. She just thinks you're too little to say it. Like you're too little for matches. You aren't, though. I used to say it all the time when I was your age." Jake said it three more times.

Destiny sat for a moment and then said it too. Slowly, as if he were tasting the sound as he said it. Then he nodded. And said it again. "I said it!" He giggled and said it again. "Just like Paulie."

Jake nodded.

"Did you burn down your school?"

"That's what they say."

"With matches?"

"Nope. I used a lighter." He pulled his lighter out of his pocket and showed it to the boy. "This one. And gasoline. In a bottle. It's called a Molotov cocktail. The school went up like a torch. Like a bomb!" He was telling the *really* bad kid story. It wasn't true, but it was no more of an exaggeration, he thought, than the story that everybody else told. Nobody had ever believed that it had all been an accident.

Destiny reached for the lighter, and Jake put it back in his pocket. "Oh no. Lighters aren't for kids."

"*You're* a kid," Destiny said.

"I'm a teenager," Jake said.

As Destiny opened his mouth to answer, the screen door burst open behind them and Randolph Applewhite came out onto the porch, a portable CD player in one hand and a briefcase in the other. Cordelia, wearing an orange skirt over her purple leotard, was right behind him. "That show is dead boring!" she was saying.

Randolph stopped, and Cordelia collided with the

CD player as he swung around to answer her. "It's the most saccharine, sentimental piece of tripe the two of them ever wrote. But it happens to be what the Traybridge Little Theatre has hired me to direct. It's the sign of a great director to be able to raise the level of the material. I intend to find a way to give the piece a new edge. People won't just be humming when they leave this production, they'll be *thinking*! It's the opportunity of a lifetime. Are you going to be part of a millennial version of a classic musical, or aren't you?"

"Why's this happening so fast? They just called you today. How come auditions are tonight?"

There was a moment of silence. When he spoke again, Randolph Applewhite's voice was tight. "They made the mistake of asking one of their board members to direct it, and he's been sent to Japan on some kind of an international currency crisis. Can you believe it? They had a *banker* directing a musical! They're lucky I happened to be between gigs."

"But what about my ballet?"

"This is a community theater production, for heaven's sake. They only rehearse in the evenings. And there's hardly any dancing in the show. It won't take you any time at all to work out the choreography, and after that I'll only need you from seven to ten P.M. You'll have all day every day to work on your ballet." He paused for a moment, frowning. "What ballet?"

Cordelia stamped her foot. "*Mine!* Where have you

been? You never listen to anybody. It's my whole fall semester project. *The Death of Ophelia.* I'm composing, playing, choreographing, dancing—everything!"

"Well, then you'll need dancers. Do this show for me and you'll have a ready-made corps de ballet, people you've already worked with."

"*I'm the dancer!* It's a one-woman ballet!"

Randolph stepped over Winston and strode down the steps past Jake and Destiny as if they weren't there. Jake had to duck to avoid being clipped in the head by the briefcase. "Just decide, Cordelia, and be quick about it. I need someone at tonight's audition to see whether these people can dance at all. If you aren't going to do it, I'll find someone who understands the importance of this opportunity."

"Oh, sure, you'll find someone by tonight. One of the many choreographers in Traybridge!"

He checked his watch. "We begin at seven, so I'll need you at the theater by six-thirty. You can take Father's car. Or Archie's truck. I'm having dinner first with that Montrose woman—the president of the board—to discuss the budget."

"Budget?" Cordelia let go of the screen door, and it crashed shut behind her. "I'd get paid?"

"I told you, this is community theater. Only the director gets paid," Randolph said as he put his briefcase and CD player into the backseat of the red Miata convertible parked in the drive.

Cordelia was left standing on the porch as the car sped down the drive, spraying gravel on the curve around the line of bushes and trees. She looked down at Jake and Destiny then, as if noticing them for the first time. She stepped over Winston and sat down on the edge of the porch, her ballet slipper–clad feet on the step next to Jake. She put her elbows on her knees and her chin in her hands. "How does he think he's going to get an edge into *The Sound of Music?*"

Jake was very much aware of how close she was sitting. *Sound of Music.* He had seen the movie once on television, but he didn't remember much about it. He remembered Julie Andrews singing in a meadow on top of a mountain. Lots of singing. And a bunch of little kids.

Destiny poked him in the ribs. "How'd you get your hair that color? And how do you make it stand up in points that way? I never saw anybody with hair that—"

Cordelia reached across in front of Jake and rapped her little brother on the head. "Don't be rude," she said.

"Ooooowww! I'm not rude. Mommy says if you want to know something you have to ask. So I asked. I don't see why it's rude to just—"

"I dyed it red," Jake said. "Bleached it first—so it looked like yours—then dyed it. But it grows in points all by itself. I can't help it. I just can't make it do anything else."

Cordelia laughed.

Destiny stuck out his lower lip. "Does not. Nobody's hair grows like that."

Before Jake could think of an answer, there was a squeal of tires from the road. The Miata careened back around the line of trees, scattering gravel in all directions. It skidded to a stop in front of the porch, and Randolph leaped out, leaving the engine running and the door open, and stormed up the front steps, forcing both Cordelia and the dog to scramble out of his way. He slammed through the screen door and was back out in less than a minute, holding a CD box over his head. "Forgot the music," he said as he pounded back to the car, got in, and slammed the door.

Meantime Jake had heard the sound of another vehicle out on the road, slowing down and changing gears as it reached the driveway to Wit's End. Randolph threw his car into reverse and backed around in front of the trees. Then he sped forward around the curve. Jake braced himself for the inevitable. There was a squeal of brakes, the sound of vehicles skidding on gravel, and then a sickening crash.

The crash was followed by a stream of curses.

"I told you that word was people talk," Jake said to Destiny.

"Sounds as if there are survivors," Cordelia said.

Chapter Seven

E.D. had gone to her room to get away from Jake for a while. She must have fallen asleep. She was jolted out of a dream about fires and explosions by the sound of the crash followed by yelling, most of which seemed to be her father. She shook the dream images from her muddled brain and left her room just in time to run into her mother, who was emerging from her office, a pencil behind each ear and her computer glasses still resting on the end of her nose.

"Where's Destiny? Has something happened to

Destiny? Somebody call 911!" she yelled.

By the time they reached the scene of the accident, it was clear that Destiny wasn't involved.

Randolph, red-faced and fairly dancing with rage, was shaking his fist at a tall, thin, pale, pimply faced young man with a ponytail, shouting about incompetent drivers and refugees from a demolition derby. The young man, his hands up as if to ward off a blow, was protesting in a high, reedy voice that he wasn't the one who'd been driving like a madman. His words were all but drowned out in a fresh deluge of verbal abuse. He kept glancing down at the thoroughly crumpled front end of an ancient and rusty Civic as if it were the battered body of a beloved family member. He looked, E.D. thought, on the brink of tears.

"Daddy's car won! Daddy's car won!" Destiny said.

It wasn't clear to E.D. that either car could be said to have won, but there was no question that the smashed bumper of the Miata, even caught as it was in the tangle of wreckage, was far less devastating to the car's future than the condition of the Civic's front end. That reminded her of an aluminum can that had been smashed for recycling. Steam was rising from beneath the mangled hood, and greenish-yellow fluid was making a puddle on the gravel. It seemed impossible that one car could be so much more damaged than the other.

Zedediah, Archie, and Lucille were converging on

the bend in the driveway from different directions, all asking questions at once. The window of Hal's room was thrown open, and his voice joined the general confusion. Winston began barking in his deepest and most threatening tone from beneath the bush where he had taken refuge.

Randolph was now threatening to bankrupt the young man with a lawsuit charging reckless driving and attempted vehicular homicide. The young man's face drained of what little color it had.

Sybil, having assured herself that Destiny was unhurt, scooped him up in her arms. Zedediah, still wearing his sawdust-covered tool apron, stepped between the two men and rested a hand on each of their shoulders. Randolph stopped shouting, and in the silence the blood gradually seemed to return to the young man's face, though he still looked ready to burst into tears.

Under Zedediah's patient questioning, the young man explained that his name was Jeremy Bernstein, he was a writer sent by a literary journal to interview Sybil Jameson, and he'd had an appointment for that evening. He had, in fact, been invited to dinner.

"No, no!" Sybil said, putting Destiny down. "That's not today! I distinctly remember that's not until the sixteenth. I invited you for the sixteenth."

"This *is* the sixteenth," Jeremy Bernstein said. Everyone else nodded in agreement.

"Can't anyone in this family keep anything straight?" Randolph said, his voice rising. "You can't just go inviting the media to descend on the household to shatter everyone's privacy. Not without at least warning the rest of us!"

E.D. could see her mother's jaw going rigid. When she spoke, it was between tightly clenched teeth. "I am immersed in what is just possibly the most important, the most difficult and complex literary work of my career. I have left the Petunia Grantham mysteries behind; I am striking out into new and unexplored territory. But do you care? Except for this young man here, I doubt that any of you even knows what I'm embarked on. I get absolutely no support from this family—I can't be expected to keep track of details!"

"Details! You can hardly call today's date a detail! It's the first sign of mental deterioration to lose track of the date." Randolph shook away his father's calming hand and looked at his watch. "This is an unmitigated catastrophe! I am supposed to have dinner with the president of the board of the Traybridge Little Theatre in exactly twenty minutes to talk about *my* work. These people are none too stable. When I don't show up on time, she's likely to panic and hire some lawyer to direct their show. Some accountant. That's what they'll do, they'll hire an accountant to direct *my* production of *The Sound of Music*." He pointed to his car. "Someone will have to take me. My car is ruined. Destroyed!"

"Don't be stupid, Randolph," Archie said. "It's nothing but the bumper and running lights that are smashed. If the headlights still pop up, we'll just rip the bumper off and you can be on your way in three minutes." He got into the car and popped up the headlights. "See? You'll be fine."

"Rip the bumper off my Miata—I have no intention of defacing this car—"

"It's already defaced. Do you want to get to your dinner or not? The way you drive, no sane person would let you borrow their car. I'll get the crowbar." Archie headed for the barn. E.D. thought he seemed particularly pleased with the idea of taking a crowbar to his brother's car.

Zedediah took a cell phone from a pocket of his tool apron, blew off the sawdust, and handed it to Randolph. "Call the restaurant and tell the woman you've been delayed."

"Yes, Randolph dear," Sybil said. "You go keep your precious appointment and leave the rest of us to clean up after you. I'm sure someone will take care of whatever we need to take care of with this young man's insurance company."

"Our lawyer will take care of that!" Randolph roared.

"We don't have a lawyer—remember? He quit after you—"

"We'll get another!"

"Fine, dear. Meantime, after you've made your call,

perhaps you'll call a tow truck to take Mr. Bernstein's car to be fixed."

Archie, who was on his way back with the crowbar, shook his head. "No point in that. It's totalled. Dead. Kaput. The condition it was in before the wreck, it's a wonder there's anything left but a handful of rust."

Now Jeremy Bernstein did burst into tears.

"Why is that man crying?" Destiny asked. "Did he get hurt in the crash? Is he going to be all right? Will he have to go to the hospital? Is he going to die? If he dies, what—"

Sybil gestured at Cordelia to take Destiny into the house. Cordelia took him by the back of the shirt, and he went, protesting all the way.

Lucille had meantime hurried to comfort the weeping young man. She patted him on the back and assured him that he could have dinner with them and that someone would take him to his hotel afterward.

"I—I don't—have—a hotel," he said, wiping his nose with the back of his hand. He took the handkerchief Zedediah offered him and blew his nose. "Thanks. I was going to find a place to stay after I'd finished the interview."

"Then you'll stay in one of the guest cottages," Lucille said. Archie had begun prying the Miata's bumper loose from the car. "E.D., please show Mr. Bernstein to Dogwood Cottage. We can deal with insurance issues in the morning."

E.D. turned and saw Jake leaning against the trunk of a tree. Winston was sitting at his feet, leaning against his legs. The look on Jake's face seemed to suggest he was actually enjoying himself. Car accidents must be right up there with fires for excitement.

Chapter Eight

Jake stared at the serving dishes on the table. Visions of starvation rose again in his mind. There was a casserole of zucchini and onions, there were sliced tomatoes, cooked carrots, green beans, beets, and a bowl of something dark green and slimy looking that Lucille identified as beet greens. "All from my garden," she told Jeremy Bernstein proudly. She didn't elaborate on nature spirits or dream communication.

When Archie came from the kitchen with a huge platter, Jake's hopes rose. There had been bacon at breakfast. These people did eat meat. But when the platter was set down in front of Zedediah, who was seated at the head of the table, Jake sighed. There were a couple of hot dogs, one bratwurst, a handful of breaded shrimp, a chicken thigh and drumstick, and a couple of indeterminate patties that might have been meat or might have been veggie burgers.

"This was it, eh?" the old man asked Archie. Archie shrugged and nodded.

"I planned a really nice dinner, honestly I did. I just thought you were coming next week," Sybil Jameson said to Bernstein. "I'm terribly sorry."

"Randolph forgot to do the grocery shopping," Archie explained as he sat down. "This was all that was left in the freezer."

Bernstein shook his head. "No problem. Honestly. No problem. I've been thinking of becoming a vegetarian anyway."

"If God had wanted humans to be vegetarians," Zedediah said, "He'd have given them cow's teeth and an extra stomach." He passed the platter down the table. "Get what you want first, young man—no telling what would be left if you waited your turn."

By the time the platter got to Jake, all that was left were the patties. Jake's stomach growled as he put one between the tiny mounds of vegetables on his plate. He wondered what sort of food was served at Juvenile Hall.

As everyone began to eat, Zedediah asked Bernstein about the magazine he wrote for.

Bernstein's eyes lit up, and he looked fully alive for the first time since he'd emerged from his ruined car. "*The New World Literary Review.* It won the Brohmer East Coast Arts Foundation award for three years in a row for its arts criticism and"—he turned to look at Sybil, who was at the end of the table opposite Zedediah—"in-depth interviews of the literary geniuses of our time. It's that sort of interview that I came to do."

"I wouldn't have thought the Petunia Grantham mysteries could get anyone classified as a literary genius," Zedediah said. "The books sell like potato chips, but—"

Bernstein choked on a bite of carrot. "Haven't you told them?" he asked Sybil. He looked around the table. "It must be difficult for the family of a writer of Ms. Jameson's stature to fully appreciate the jewel they have in their midst. The Petunia Grantham mysteries are splendid examples of their genre, of course. But our readers are getting a sneak preview of her *new* work. The first two chapters of what will no doubt be heralded as the literary masterpiece of the new century will be printed in the next issue. I've been sent to do the interview that will accompany those chapters. Everyone at the *Review* is terrifically excited. It's an event of enormous interest to the whole literary community when a writer as popular as Ms. Jameson stakes out new artistic territory. The world is awaiting the coming Great American Novel with bated breath."

"It must be getting blue in the face by this time," Cordelia said. "If it's the book she started when I was in kindergarten, the world's been waiting for this particular Great American Novel for more than ten years."

"And well worth the wait," Bernstein said, "judging from the opening chapters, which I've been privileged to read. One can't rush a work of art."

"Who would have guessed that Debbie Applewhite would turn into a literary genius before our eyes," Zedediah said.

"Debbie Applewhite?"

"Zedediah!" Sybil said, her face flushing red. She turned to Bernstein. "That's off the record! I've been Sybil Jameson for nearly twenty years. My parents named me Debbie. For Debbie Reynolds. I can't imagine what they were thinking of."

"But he said Applewhite?"

"My married name, of course."

Jeremy Bernstein looked from Sybil to Zedediah and back again, his eyes at least twice as big as normal. "Applewhite? Your married name is Applewhite! Then your husband, the man who crashed into me—the man I crashed into—is Randolph Applewhite? The theater director?"

"You've heard of him?"

"I reviewed his off-Broadway revival of *Time Remembered* for my college newspaper! It was magnificent. Randolph Applewhite. I didn't realize. I didn't—" Bernstein stopped and looked back at Zedediah. His eyes, Jake thought, looked about to pop out of his head. "Applewhite. Zedediah Applewhite? Of Zedediah Applewhite handcrafted wood furniture?"

Zedediah nodded.

"Good heavens! And Lucille—Archie—"

"It's quite a clan," Zedediah said.

"Lucille Applewhite, the poet! This is so amazing. I own both of your chapbooks. And Archie Applewhite—I've visited your website. And I saw your *Chair with Ottoman* in a gallery just last month. It was stunning. So original and inventive."

"I hope you had the good sense not to try to sit on it," Archie said.

"Applewhite. Jameson. I had no idea. No one at the *Review* had any idea." Bernstein put his hand over his heart and took a deep breath. His cheeks had gone pink. "I apologize for my ignorance. I'm so embarrassed. I had no idea that all the Applewhites were the same family. Or that Sybil Jameson was—"

"An Applewhite as well—by marriage of course," Zedediah said. "As patriarch of this clan I can't really take credit for her—or Lucille, for that matter. Except that my sons had the good sense to choose them."

"I'm an Applewhite!" Destiny said. "My name's Destiny Applewhite. Destiny is my first name and—"

"But this is too wonderful!" Bernstein said. "An artistic dynasty. Like the painters . . . ah . . . um . . . you know . . . the Wyeths! Or the writing Brontës. Or the acting Barrymores. Except that you each do such different work." He turned back to Sybil. "You never gave so much as a hint."

Sybil was sitting very still. When she spoke, her voice was chilly. "I was under the impression that you were coming to interview me. It didn't occur to me to mention my family. Any more than it would have occurred to any of them to mention me."

"Ah!" Bernstein said. "Yes, well." He cleared his throat. "But I have to tell you it's exciting to be sitting here at a table in the midst of so much talent. It's like expecting to find a diamond and stumbling into an entire mine. The children? Do they—"

"The children are still exploring their artistic potentials," Sybil said. "Destiny shows signs of talent in the visual arts. He has a real eye for color."

"That's me, Destiny," Destiny said. "I gots lots and lots of finger paintings. You want to see my finger paintings?" He got down from the table and went off toward the schoolroom.

Sybil went on. "Hal, whom you haven't met—"

"Nor are likely to, unless you're planning to put down roots," Archie said. "None of us has laid eyes on him for months."

Sybil frowned at Archie. "Hal is something of an introvert, but I'm sure you understand the sensitive artistic temperament." Bernstein nodded, his face serious and sympathetic. "He was passionately into painting for a while, but judging from the new sign on his door, the materials he's been ordering on the Internet, and the sounds coming from his room, he seems to be expanding his range. We all respect his artistic privacy, of course, so we won't know what he's working on until he's ready to show us."

"*I'm* composing and choreographing an original ballet," Cordelia said. "I also play the music and will dance it. It's a solo ballet called *The Death of Ophelia.* From *Hamlet,* you know."

"Ah. Ophelia. Unrequited love, madness, drowning! Superb material for a ballet. An opera even."

"I don't sing."

"That's the Achilles heel of the whole Applewhite clan," Zedediah said. "If there's a singing gene, we don't have it. Applewhites don't sing."

"I do!" Destiny had come back in, carrying a large sheet of paper covered with red and green smudges. "I sing all the time." He put down his finger painting and launched into "The Itsy-Bitsy Spider" at the top of his lungs, walking his fingers up an imaginary waterspout. Destiny proved Zedediah's point, Jake thought.

From then on the conversation went on around

Jake so fast and furiously that he wasn't sure he could have followed it if he'd wanted to. It was all about art. Mostly Applewhite art. He did his best, in spite of his total loathing of cooked vegetables, to eat enough to keep body and soul together, slipping bits of zuchini and beet and cooked carrot to the dog at his feet under the table. Though he was apparently willing to eat anything, Winston seemed to enjoy beet greens in particular.

"You're very lucky to be invited to participate in this amazing educational opportunity," Bernstein said to Jake at one point. Jake realized the conversation had come around to the Creative Academy. He nodded dutifully. He hadn't been listening, so he didn't know whether Bernstein understood why he'd been "invited to participate."

"You know," Bernstein went on, addressing the whole family now, "I have a friend who's a producer for a magazine show on one of the television networks. He's always looking for stories with enough of a hook to interest the network executives. I've never had one to give him before, but I think this could be it. The Applewhite artistic dynasty and the home school designed to perpetuate it. If I may borrow a computer, I could e-mail him the idea tonight. I know it would be an invasion of your privacy, but I think those of us who understand the importance of the arts owe it to the rest of America to give them a taste of what it's all about."

Later, while Bernstein and the adults carried the conversation into the living room and Cordelia put Destiny to bed, Jake and E.D. were sent to rinse the dishes and put them in the dishwasher. E.D. said nothing at all as they worked, but she crashed plates and glasses into each other so ferociously, Jake was surprised that nothing broke. What's her problem? Jake wondered, setting the meat platter on the floor for Winston to lick.

Chapter Nine

E.D. slammed the door to her room and threw herself on the bed. *Not one word!* she thought. Neither her mother nor Zedediah had said a single word about her to Jeremy Bernstein. Her name hadn't even been mentioned. She might as well have been in Traybridge with her father! Invisible, that's what she was. The invisible Applewhite. It was too much. She wanted out of this family.

She turned over and lay on her back, staring up at the posters of rock stars she had taped to the ceiling. Cordelia and Hal didn't have posters of rock stars.

They wouldn't sink so low as to admit they liked what almost every other kid their age in the whole civilized world liked. Oh no. They were much too individual for that. Much too artsy. And that wimpy Jeremy Bernstein probably never had rock stars on his ceiling either. He probably had posters of Shakespeare or Picasso or—or—Edith Wharton!

Well, she had news for her family. She might not have a talent that would get a television producer excited about doing a story on her. But *she* wouldn't lose track of the date or forget to go to the grocery when they were out of food. Unlike certain other people, she was going to be able to cope with the real world when she got old enough to go out into it on her own.

The way Jeremy Bernstein had talked about the Creative Academy, anybody would have thought the adults had thought it up specifically to educate the next generation of artistic geniuses. The truth was, she was the only one who was doing anything to keep it any sort of *school* at all, the only one actually getting an education from it, and the only one making sure that Destiny would get an education.

She had read somewhere that the best way to learn something was to teach it, so she had built in a Teaching Opportunities section to every single project in her curriculum. When she'd learned enough about each project, she taught the main ideas to

Destiny. That way he was learning a whole bunch of things he might never decide to learn on his own, and he was learning them really early, before he was even supposed to be a student in the academy, so that when he began doing his own thing, whatever that turned out to be, he wouldn't end up as ignorant as Cordelia and Hal were bound to be.

Jeremy Bernstein was worried about a television show invading their family's privacy. That just showed how little he understood them. Every last one of them lived to be the center of attention. Even Hal. Turning himself into a recluse guaranteed that people would talk about him.

She threw her extra pillow across the room. She *hated* being an Applewhite.

Chapter Ten

According to the alarm clock on his bedside table, it was 5:03 A.M. when Jake woke to the shrieking clatter of an electric coffee grinder. He buried his head under the pillow and turned over to go back to sleep. But now that he was awake, he had to go to the bathroom. When he opened the door of his bedroom, he saw Archie, dressed in jogging clothes and bustling around the cottage's small kitchen area. Jake nodded in his direction but didn't return Archie's greeting. How could anyone have that much good cheer at that hour of the morning? Lucille had called Archie a lark. True. Nobody but birds was up at this hour.

Or so he thought. He had just gone back to bed and was slipping happily into a dream about a spectacularly beautiful dancer in a purple leotard when something thundered across the room and landed on him like a mortar round, knocking the breath out of him. He felt the covers being pulled off his head.

"You are so too awake! Uncle Archie said you was asleep. He said you didn't even wake up when you went to the bathroom before. You isn't asleep at all. You gots your eyes open and everything!"

Groaning, Jake maneuvered so that Destiny's weight slid off his stomach and onto the edge of the bed. Then he pushed himself up to his elbows. The boy, dressed in pirate pajamas, did not stop talking.

"Your hair points is all messed and flat. I told you! Nobody gots hair that grows in points like you said. You gots to do something to it to make it do that. I wanna watch you do it. Can I watch? Can I? Huh? Can I?"

"No!" Jake said. "Go away. I'm not ready to be awake yet. I'm *not* awake."

"Are so. You gots your eyes open and you're talking. Jake's awake, Jake's awake, Jake's awake!"

"Go home. Don't you know you're not supposed to barge into somebody's bedroom without knocking?"

Destiny jumped off the bed, ran to the open door, and knocked on it. "I knocked. Now do I gets to watch you make your hair do points? Can I, can I, can I?"

"Destiny! What did I tell you?" Archie appeared in the doorway. He shook his head at Jake. "You might as well get up. I could take him away, but he'll come back. Believe me, you're better off getting up now. And here's somebody who followed him over." Winston came into the room, jumped heavily up onto Jake's bed, and licked him on the nose.

"Okay! Okay! I give up." The prospect of life at Juvenile Hall was beginning to seem tempting.

Jake took a shower, listening to what seemed like two hundred repetitions of "*Frère Jacques,*" which could be heard even over the sound of the water running. He got dressed and then let Destiny sit on the edge of the tub while he gelled and combed his hair into its all-over porcupine points. It was somehow a lot harder to do with somebody watching. Winston lay on the damp bath mat, his nose between his paws, his eyes focused on Jake as if the jar of gel were something to eat.

Archie stuck his head in to tell them he was off to jog and do his morning Tai Chi. "You can have breakfast here if you like—there's cereal. Or go up to the main house and see what's there, if anything. Somebody else is bound to be up in a couple of hours."

Destiny begged Jake to gel and spike his hair, too, but Jake had no intention of becoming a hairdresser for a four-year-old. He told Destiny that, even with the gel, only teenage hair would stay up in points.

"Little-kid hair won't do that."

When Jake had finished his hair, Lucille still didn't seem to be up. Jake wasn't used to being up, dressed, and ready for the day at this hour. He told Destiny to go back to the main house and take Winston with him, but that was like telling a tidal wave to turn around and go back out to sea. So he went into the kitchen and looked through the cupboards till he found a box of Cheerios and two bowls. "You can eat with me," he told Destiny, who was singing "Pop Goes the Weasel" now, "but after that, you have to go up to the house and get dressed. You don't want to spend the day in pajamas."

Destiny stopped singing long enough to say that he could spend the day in pajamas if he wanted to and sometimes he did.

Jake sighed. It wouldn't be possible for Destiny to grow up to be a delinquent—there didn't seem to be any rules for him to break.

The only milk in the refrigerator was in a canning jar. He poured it on both bowls of Cheerios. When he put the first spoonful into his mouth, he spit it right back into his spoon. "What's the matter with this milk?" he said.

Destiny, chewing a mouthful perfectly cheerfully, shrugged. "It's from the goatses," he said when he'd swallowed.

Jake's Cheerios went to Winston.

Chapter Eleven

In the schoolroom E.D. was getting ready for the day's work. She was going to start the Teaching Opportunities part of the Butterfly Project because it would give Jake something to do that didn't involve any interaction with living creatures. If he didn't want to cooperate, it wouldn't be her fault. She'd brought a gallon jug of water, a bucket, a box of wheat paste, and a stack of newspapers to tear. She was going to make a papier-mâché caterpillar and chrysalis to teach Destiny about metamorphosis.

Jake, his earphones pushed back on his head, was slouched at his desk now with Winston at his feet, doing his best to fend off Destiny's eternal questions. "What kinda stuff did you puts on your hair to make it red? Paint? How come you did red? Could you make it green instead? Could you make it blue or purple or silver?" E.D. remembered a nature documentary she'd seen where a male lion was being tormented by a cub who bit his tail and pounced on his back and chewed on his ears. Eventually the lion had swatted the cub with one huge paw and sent it tumbling. She hoped her father, who was the teacher on call today, would get here before Jake got fed up enough with Destiny to do any swatting. Her father was late. It was already almost nine-thirty.

She was just pouring the water into the bucket when Randolph appeared in the schoolroom doorway in pajamas and slippers, his hair disheveled and his eyes screwed up against the daylight. "Awful night," he said. "Didn't get a wink of sleep." He peered at Jake. "We're supposed to be keeping an eye on you till you get adjusted, but you're just going to have to work on your own today. You do have something you can do, right?"

Jake shrugged.

"Good. Good. Excellent." Randolph reached over and grabbed the earphones off Jake's head. Jake swore as Randolph pulled the wire loose from his

Walkman, but Randolph paid no attention. "These things'll make you deaf by the time you're twenty."

Randolph put the earphones around his neck and then rubbed his face with both hands as he turned to E.D. "The audition was a disaster. A raging disaster! You'd be amazed at how many stage mothers there are in a town the size of Traybridge. Unfortunately none of their kids has a shred of talent. And the adults! I'm not insisting on a Julie Andrews or a Mary Martin, but it would be nice to have one or two people who can sing *and* act, preferably at the same time. I'll be on the phone all day, calling everyone who's ever directed a musical in this state, trying to locate some—within driving distance, if possible. Thanks to Cordelia, I have to find a dance person, too. I gave her an opportunity to participate in what could be the best piece of musical theater ever produced in this county, and she turned me down cold. How sharper than a serpent's tooth is an ungrateful child!"

He started away and then turned back. "Where's that wretched little road menace who destroyed my car? And why hasn't the tow truck come to drag away that piece of junk he was driving? It looks like someone's had a demolition derby in our front yard."

"He's in Dogwood Cottage," E.D. said. "Grandpa said he could deal with his car today."

"He'd better have himself a first-rate lawyer if he

wants to get out of this with a penny in his pocket." He left, muttering under his breath about reckless driving. E.D. was starting to stir the wheat paste into the water when he put his head back through the doorway. "If you *really* need anything this morning, you can come and get me. If you *really* need it." He blinked at Jake once or twice. "Independence. That's what the Creative Academy is all about. Independence! Remember that." Then he was gone.

"I'll bet you never went to a school before where the teachers were too busy to hang out in the classroom with the students," E.D. said to Jake.

"He stole my earphones!" Jake said. "He can't do that."

"He already did." She turned to Destiny, who was talking about hair colors again. If no adult was going to protect the cub from the lion, she'd have to. "Destiny, you go find today's newspaper and bring it to me, and I'll set you up with your fingerpaints when you get back."

Destiny went off humming to himself, and E.D. handed Jake her curriculum notebook. "I don't see how you're going to catch up with any of this, but if you aren't planning to go to Juvenile Hall, you might as well do something. *Butterflies of the Carolinas* is over there on the computer desk. And there are a couple of butterfly websites you can check out."

Jake set the notebook on his desk. "I can catch up

whenever I feel like it. I never got expelled for being *dumb*."

"That depends on how smart you think it was to land yourself here." She tossed him some newspapers. "If you don't want to read about butterflies, you can tear strips."

"Tear strips?"

"Newspaper strips." She explained about the papier-mâché caterpillar, about Teaching Opportunities.

"What kind of caterpillar is it supposed to be?" He looked at the chart on the wall. "Better make it a great spangled fritillary, since you haven't caught one."

"The caterpillar I'm making is a monarch," she said stiffly. "It has the prettiest chrysalis. But I *will* catch a fritillary."

"Pretty sure of yourself."

"I'll catch one!"

When Destiny brought back the paper, E.D. spread it on the floor in the corner of the room and set him up with some huge pieces of shiny white paper, a bowl of water, and a box of fingerpaints. Before she let him start, she buttoned a paint-smeared man's shirt onto him backward so that it hung like a dress from his chin to his ankles. He settled happily and began to work, smearing not only the paper, but the shirt and sometimes his face with color. As he painted, he talked steadily to himself, to the paint, to the paper. When he wasn't talking, he was repeating nonsense syllables over and over again, in a sort of singsong chant. "You get used to it," E.D. told Jake. "After a while you won't notice him anymore—like the sound of a refrigerator turning on and off."

Jake, still slouched, began tearing strips of paper, and E.D. started to work on the caterpillar. By the time she was finished, Jake was reading *Butterflies of the Carolinas*. She wiped her hands on a rag and told him she would take the caterpillar out in the sun to dry. "Then I'm going to go catch a fritillary." Destiny was earnestly telling himself about the big orange tiger he was about to paint in the green, green jungle. "You can keep an eye on Destiny."

She took Jake's lack of response as agreement, grabbed the butterfly net, and left. There were no fritillaries in the meadow. There were only a couple of summer azures and an orange sulphur. It couldn't be getting too late in the season. It was only past the middle of September. She could feel her stomach getting more and more knotted as she pushed her way through the shoulder-high stalks of goldenrod. What if she *didn't* find a fritillary? She hated the idea of leaving a space in the Butterfly Project without a check mark. Worse, she'd told Jake she would catch a fritillary. She absolutely *had* to!

She was just about to give up when an orange-and-beige butterfly of the right size flew out from behind a tulip tree at the edge of the meadow. It landed on a spray of goldenrod, its wings closed so that she couldn't see the markings. She crept closer, the net ready in her hand. As she was about to sweep the net to catch it, the butterfly opened its wings and fluttered away. E.D. bit her lip to keep from crying with disappointment. The markings were soft and brown, not black. It was a fritillary all right, but not a great spangled. Three different times she'd caught a variegated fritillary. She knew the difference by this time. Sweaty and furious, she stayed out awhile longer, but finally had to head back. She didn't want to leave Destiny with Jake for too long.

As she got close to the house, she saw Jake coming from the direction of the dance studio. Winston was waddling along with him. Destiny wasn't with them. Beneath the sound of hammering that came from Hal's room, she could just make out the music for Cordelia's ballet. Jake must have been watching her again.

"You were supposed to be keeping an eye on Destiny," she told him as he joined her.

"Independence," he said. "That's what the Creative Academy is all about!"

"Destiny's only four!"

"A pretty independent four if you ask me. I told him I didn't think he was independent enough to finish the painting he was working on all by himself. He said he could prove he was. So I let him."

"It's never a good idea to leave Destiny alone."

"Didn't get your fritillary, huh?" He was smirking at her.

"I'll get it!" she said.

When they got to the schoolroom, Destiny greeted them at the door. "Look at me! Look at me!" His hair, slathered with wheat paste, stood up in clumps and tufts all over his head. "See, Jake? Little-kid hair does so too stand up in points. When it's all dry, I'm gonna paint it purple! Or green. I like green. Do you like green?"

Chapter Twelve

A week later, Jake stood in the bathroom of Wisteria Cottage, humming abstractedly to himself as he gelled his hair into points. He frowned into the mirror. He'd taken on this look so long ago that he could hardly remember himself any other way. But the truth was he was getting tired of doing this every day. It was one thing to go to so much trouble when people took notice, when it got him something he wanted. But here it didn't get him anything at all. Nobody cared. The only Applewhite who even noticed his hair anymore was

Destiny. And that had gotten to be a major pain.

The day with the wheat paste Destiny had absolutely insisted on letting his hair dry that way, though Jake and E.D. had kept him from painting it. Jake understood, now, why wheat paste was used to do papier-mâché. When it dried, it was like rock. Sybil Jameson had refused to take any motherly responsibility for the situation at all. "You're the one who gave him the idea in the first place," she told Jake. "You wash the stuff out." Jake had never handled a screaming, flailing four-year-old before. It had taken an hour and a half of head soaking and hysteria to get all the wheat paste out, and by that time Jake had been as wet and exhausted as Destiny.

That had been only the beginning. The next day Destiny had painted his hair with green fingerpaint. The day after that he'd used colored markers to give it rainbow stripes. Luckily, they were watercolor ones. Destiny was so prone to coloring things that weren't meant to be colored that permanent markers had been banned from the Applewhite household altogether.

Nobody minded the boy spending the day with vividly colored hair, but Sybil insisted the color be washed out before bed. Jake, of course, had to do it. And Destiny had turned it into a game to see how hard he could make it for Jake to get the job done. Very hard! The kid was incorrigible. What the

Applewhites ought to do, Jake thought, was shave Destiny's head!

Jake stared at his own hair. It was getting too long for this. Besides, the dark brown roots were showing now in a way that was starting to look scruffy instead of intentional. Then there was the problem of his clothes. It was hot out. Sunny and hot and humid. Black clothes made it seem even hotter. And black clothes were the only clothes he owned. He'd worn the spiked collar only twice—it had made his neck sweat and then chafed it raw.

Jake was beginning to feel he was disappearing altogether. Nobody except E.D. and Destiny noticed when he swore. Destiny giggled and E.D. just sighed and shook her head. Nothing he'd done before to show people who he was and what he stood for worked here.

He couldn't even chill out the way he used to. No TV to watch. His Walkman was useless without earphones. If he dared to smoke where he could be seen, somebody was sure to snatch away his cigarette. It wasn't only Zedediah who did it. Archie had, and Lucille, too. Archie only snatched and stomped, but Lucille had delivered a ten-minute lecture—not on the dangers of cigarette smoking, which he'd heard about a zillion times before, but on the desecration of tobacco, which she said was sacred to American Indian spirituality. By the end of the lecture she'd worked herself into tears about the "wanton destruction of native culture in the Americas." Lucille Applewhite was such an incredibly cheerful person it was actually painful to see her in tears. It wasn't the sort of feeling Jake was used to.

So he'd taken one of his last cigarettes out into the meadow three days ago to find a place to smoke it in peace. There'd been no place to sit in the meadow. He'd found a log by the edge of the pond and settled himself there. Winston had gone along with him, and Jake had no sooner lit his cigarette and taken a nice, long, relaxing drag than the dog got himself stuck in the mud by the cattails and started howling as if he were being murdered. When Jake went to pull him out, he got stuck, too. It was the smelliest, blackest, most disgusting mud he'd ever encountered, and it snatched one of his sneakers right off his foot. By the time he'd managed to crawl out, drag the dog free, and find his sneaker, he was muck from neck to toe.

Later, he'd found two ticks on the back of his neck, their heads buried in his skin, sucking his blood. Archie had pulled them off with tweezers and assured him that he wasn't *likely* to get Rocky Mountain spotted fever, since the ticks hadn't been on him long enough, but the ordeal had wrecked the whole idea of sneaking off for a relaxing smoke.

Apart from the pond incident, the dog was getting to be a real nuisance. Where Jake went, Winston went. He had abandoned the main house altogether and taken up residence in Wisteria Cottage. More specifically in Jake's room. Though Jake insisted the dog sleep on the lavender braided rug, when he woke in the morning at the horrible predawn hour when Archie ground his coffee before going out for his morning exercise, Winston was invariably lying alongside him, pinning him beneath the covers, snoring steadily and drooling on his pillow. He had to shove the dog off the bed if he had to get up to go to the bathroom.

Now Jake finished his hair, stepped back, and tripped over Winston, who was lying behind him. The dog yelped and leaped to his feet so that Jake stumbled over him again, cracking his elbow on the sink and his knee on the toilet before he got his balance. He swore. "What's the matter with you, dog? Why can't you just leave me alone?" Winston stared up at him with those sad, droopy eyes and wagged his tail. The overwhelming impulse to boot the dog out into the hall vanished. Jake reached down and rubbed the dog behind his ears. *There. That proved it.* The Jake he knew, the Jake he had always been, was disappearing. And there was nothing—nobody—to put in his place.

Chapter Thirteen

E.D. was alone in the schoolroom, sitting at the computer with her hands pressed over her ears. Jake and his canine shadow, Winston, had gone into Traybridge with Archie to get some supplies for the wood shop, and Lucille had taken Destiny along to the library. Jeremy Bernstein was still staying in Dogwood Cottage. He had decided to write a book about what he insisted on calling the Applewhite Artistic Dynasty, and he had been practically monopolizing the schoolroom computer, working on the book and exchanging e-mails with his TV friend, trying to arrange a documentary about them all, or a story on a magazine show at least. But he was out in the wood shop now. It was a chance to get online and do her math. Except that she couldn't concentrate.

E.D. had always thought you could get used to sounds, the way you got used to smells after a while. *Sensory fatigue*, it was called. You would get so you didn't notice anymore. Like Destiny's nonstop chatter. She'd told Jake it was like getting used to a refrigerator motor. And she'd been right. Everybody got used to Destiny. You couldn't survive in this family otherwise.

But this was different. This was worse. Much, much worse. This was torture. She'd heard somewhere that when the cops or the FBI or somebody had wanted to end a siege with a militant cult, they'd beamed rock and roll music at them from high-powered speakers. She could understand why it would work. Only they shouldn't have used rock and roll. They should have used *The Sound of Music*. It would have been faster. After twenty-four hours the people in the cult would have laid down their guns and come out on their hands and knees, eyes as crazed as Wolfie's, singing compulsively about female deer and kitten whiskers.

For five days now her father had been playing the CD of *The Sound of Music* all day, every day. He said he needed to totally immerse himself in the musical ambiance of the show. So *everybody* was being totally immersed in the musical ambiance of the show. Her mother had begged him to use earphones, but he refused, of course. "They not only destroy your eardrums, they mess up your brain waves!" So the music blared out from the living room speakers, not just through the whole of the main house, but out the open windows and all over Wit's End.

Upstairs Hal had gone almost silent for a while after the UPS man dropped off a roll of chicken wire and two gigantic bags of plaster. The sign on his door that had once read HAL APPLEWHITE, PAINTER now said HAL APPLEWHITE, SCULPTOR. But whatever he was sculpting with chicken wire and plaster, Hal had taken up hammering again. Purely, E.D. thought, in self-defense. Sybil had turned up the volume on the white noise machine in her office and had taken to wearing earmuffs in order to keep writing her Great American Novel.

Cordelia swore the sound carried out to the dance studio. Her ballet, she claimed, was changing from a discordant tragedy to something resembling a polka. Most days Lucille stayed in Wisteria Cottage with all the doors and windows closed and the curtains drawn. She said it was the only way she could write poetry that didn't fall into rhymes like *thread* and *bread*, *mitten* and *kitten*. E.D. figured it was the music that had sent Jeremy Bernstein out to the wood shop.

He could do interviews with Zedediah and Archie out there, where the power tools overwhelmed any other sounds.

It wasn't that E.D. didn't like the music. She did. But the constant repetition had worn grooves in her brain. Even in those few blessed hours when Randolph took the CD and went off to Traybridge for what he called his "eternal, unending, utterly futile auditions," there was no respite. The music kept playing over and over in her mind. She would catch herself humming it. Whistling it. It wasn't just the hills that were alive with this music, it was the trees, the grass, the house, the universe! Even worse, Jake had taken to humming it as well, so that if she did manage to drive it out of her mind briefly, he might bring it rushing back at any moment.

Randolph Applewhite didn't very often direct musicals, and when he did, he usually went somewhere else to do it. Some other city in some other state. If he ever got this show cast and if the family survived the rehearsal period, E.D. was going to suggest they make a family rule against his ever again directing a musical from home.

Partly to get away from the music and partly because it had become an obsession, E.D. had spent a good part of the week in the meadow, by the pond, in the pine grove, anywhere and everywhere on their sixteen acres—looking for a great spangled fritillary.

When she came back each day, the unused camera on its strap around her neck, her net empty, Jake's smirk seemed to get bigger and broader. E.D. didn't give up easily, but she was beginning to lose hope. September was the last month they were supposed to be out there, and they were listed as rare during the second half of the month. There were only six more days in September.

It was beginning to look likely that the Butterfly Project would end with a gaping hole in the chart. It drove her nuts. The great spangled fritillary was a *common* butterfly. The book said so. She should have found one weeks ago. It was just some nasty twist of fate that she hadn't found one. It was like a curse. If Jake Semple hadn't come into her life, she was absolutely certain she would have found one by now. But he had come, and then he'd challenged her. She'd told him that she *would* find one, and now if she didn't, Jake Semple would win!

Everything else about the project was finished. The papier-mâché caterpillar and chrysalis were sitting on a shelf in the schoolroom, painted according to the pictures in her book, and she'd scheduled the Teaching Opportunity about metamorphosis for the first of next week. She was going to explain to Destiny how the caterpillar turned itself into the chrysalis and then she would cut the chrysalis open and explain how the monarch butterfly that she had a photograph of on the chart had climbed out of it and flown away. The Teaching Opportunity and a paper describing the project and its results were what she called the Culminating Events. Her paper was almost done—it was just waiting for a paragraph on the great spangled fritillary or else the statement that she had had to give up on finding one. A statement of defeat she couldn't bear to think about.

There were no official grades at the Creative Academy, but E.D. always graded herself on her projects. It gave her a sense of where she was, what she had done, and most of the time a comforting feeling of accomplishment. But without the great spangled fritillary, she was going to have to give herself a B in science for the first half of this term. She was not used to getting Bs. She worked and worked until she felt sure she had earned an A. This fritillary thing wasn't something she could do by hard work. It was totally out of her control.

Worse, she'd been so determined to find one that she had fallen behind in every other subject. Including math. Her math tutor had sent her an e-mail asking if she was sick. She was doing her best to catch up now. But the more she tried to concentrate, the more she was aware of the voice singing "Climb Ev'ry Mountain." It filled the house, urging her to climb mountains, ford streams, follow rainbows.

Suddenly a new voice joined the one pouring out of

the living room speakers. Jake burst into the schoolroom singing at the top of his lungs that she should keep climbing and fording and following. Mercifully, when the final chord had died away, the CD ended and the house was suddenly silent. Hal's hammering stopped with the music. Jake stood there smirking, his hands behind his back. Winston had come in after him and now flopped at his feet. "The song's right!" Jake said.

"About what?"

"About finding your dream if you look hard enough. Well, I wouldn't call it a dream exactly—not mine anyway—and there weren't any mountains involved. But I found it!" With that he brought out from behind his back a clear plastic box like the kind nuts and bolts come in. Lying in the box, its wings battered, its body shriveled, was a great spangled fritillary.

"You killed it!" she said.

"It was dead when I found it. Guess where!" When she didn't guess, he told her anyway. "Stuck to the front of Archie's truck. Inside the grille. It must have been there for days. Maybe even weeks."

E.D. stared at the battered insect. There was no mistaking what it was.

She wanted to cry. This was almost as bad as ending with a hole on the chart. The Butterfly Project would get an A now. But it wouldn't really be her A. It would belong to both of them.

Chapter Fourteen

What's the matter with the girl? Jake thought. He'd saved her stupid project for her, hadn't he? So why was she pissed off? She should have been grateful. All the way back from Traybridge he'd imagined her reaction to his finding the lousy butterfly she wanted, and he might just as well have brought her a slug. A toad. A road-killed possum. That's what he got for trying to be nice. Well, he wouldn't let it happen again!

Jake slammed the plastic box down on E.D.'s desk

as Randolph Applewhite burst into the schoolroom and stumbled over Winston, who was lying across the doorway. Winston yelped and scrambled out of the way, but Randolph barely seemed to notice. "Who was that singing? Who was that singing?" He looked wildly around the schoolroom. "Jake? That can't have been you. Was it? Was that *you*?"

Jake shrugged. "Just now? I—I guess so. I was just singing along with—"

"Where did you learn to sing? And where did you get that magnificent voice?"

"I don't know—I just—"

"Never mind. Can you act?"

Jake shrugged again. He had played a pumpkin in a first-grade Thanksgiving play, but it hadn't required any acting. His teacher had given him the part because it didn't have any lines. She had been afraid of what he might say if he was allowed to speak onstage.

"We'll find out tonight. You'll come to auditions, and I'll have you read with Jeannie Ng. She's the only person I've seen or heard yet who could possibly play Liesl." Randolph took hold of Jake's shoulders and looked at him intently, his head cocked to one side. "Possible. Just possible. Luckily, Jeannie's really small. Do you know Rolf's song?"

"Rolf's—?"

E.D. said, "Rolf? Jake can't play Rolf! Rolf's seventeen years old."

"I know, I know—going on eighteen. You're—how old, Jake?"

"Thirteen. Last May."

"Well, thank heavens your voice has changed already. And you're tall for your age. Rolf could be small. It doesn't say anywhere Rolf can't be small. All the more reason he would want to join the SS—to make up for being a runt. The psychology of it's perfect." Randolph let go of him then. "It's an excellent part. A wonderful song, a little dancing, a romantic interest. And you'd get to be the source of all the onstage tension at the end."

"But I've never—"

"Doesn't matter. You can sing! You have a strong, powerful voice and you stay on key. Right now I wouldn't care if you couldn't act your way out of a paper bag. You're smart enough. If you can't act, I'll teach you. I'll get you a script right away. In all these interminable auditions I haven't found a single person who could come close to playing Rolf. Not one. And here you were all the time, right under my nose!"

With that Randolph Applewhite left the schoolroom, humming Rolf's song to himself, slightly off-key. A good thing he doesn't have to teach singing, Jake thought.

"Are you going to do it?" E.D. asked.

"What's it to you?" Jake said. It was a question Jake should have been asking himself. But for some reason he wasn't. Randolph Applewhite wanted him to be in

The Sound of Music. From the very moment he'd understood that, Jake had known the answer. Of course he was going to do it.

"Because if you do, and if you dare—*dare*—to sing Rolf's song, or any other one for that matter, even once in this room while I'm trying to work, I'll—I'll—"

Jake wasn't listening, he was thinking. His heart, he noticed suddenly, was actually pounding with excitement. He'd never auditioned for anything. What if he froze up? And what would it be like to sing on a stage in front of a lot of people? He'd never done it before. Then there was the acting. He didn't know for certain that he could act, at least not with a script and lines somebody else made up. But something told him he could. Now that he thought about it, acting was what he'd been doing all his life.

He didn't know the show, really, but he knew the music. By now there wasn't anybody at Wit's End who didn't know every word to every single song. Randolph had asked where Jake had learned to sing. The weird thing was that until this very moment, he hadn't even known he could. Not really. *Magnificent,* Randolph Applewhite had called his voice. *Magnificent.*

Chapter Fifteen

Her father hadn't been gone two minutes before Jake started humming Rolf's song. E.D. shut down the computer and stormed out of the schoolroom, her stomach churning. She had just started up the stairs to her room when the CD began again and the house filled with the opening notes of *The Sound of Music*'s overture. Almost immediately the hammering started up in Hal's room.

E.D. turned and went out through the kitchen, slamming the screen door behind her. Under the big beech tree near the barn, Lucille was reading to Destiny. Paulie, from the porch of her grandfather's cottage, was shrieking with maniacal laughter, and the strains of Ophelia's death ballet drifted up from the dance studio. These sounds, along with the high, vibrant thrum of cicadas, seemed almost to collide inside her skull with the music from the house.

Now that she was out here, she didn't know what she wanted to do. There was no need to get the butterfly net and head out to the meadow. There were no more butterflies to find. And she couldn't do any other work unless she went back to the schoolroom first to get her materials. Right now she didn't care whether she ever went back to the schoolroom again. She didn't know *why* she was feeling the way she was feeling. For that matter, she didn't know what she was feeling. But she didn't care. Whatever it was, it was awful, and she wanted to make it go away.

She kept walking till she found herself at the goat pen. Wolfie had to be in the shed. Only Hazel was outside. She was in the corner of the pen, her head under the bottom rail, her neck stretched as far as it would go, trying to reach a clump of weeds on the other side. Not so much as a blade of grass was growing inside the pen. The goats had stripped it clean. Their food trough was empty. E.D. pulled up the clump of weeds by the roots and tossed it over the fence. Hazel pulled her head free, picked up the weeds, and began munching. E.D. decided to get a scoop of feed for her and had just put one hand on the gate when Wolfie came thundering out of the shed, eyes blazing, head down. He tore past Hazel and crashed into the gate so hard the impact jolted E.D.'s arm clear to her shoulder.

"Fine!" she said to the goat, who had now snatched the weeds from Hazel and was shaking them from side to side as if killing them. "You can just starve for all I care. Both of you!"

The lathe started up in the wood shop. E.D. followed the sound like a trail of bread crumbs. Maybe hanging out with Zedediah for a while would make her feel better. Zedediah could always make her feel better.

"Whoa, Nellie," her grandfather said over the sound of the lathe as she slipped in through the door, "who skunked *your* dog?"

"What?"

He turned off the machine. "I haven't seen anything as threatening as the expression on your face since I saw a tornado heading for the highway while I was driving back from the coast in a hurricane."

There were three newly finished rocking chairs in the shop. E.D. threw herself into one of them. "Where's Archie?"

"Is he the one you're mad at?"

"No. I mean I'm not *mad* at anybody."

Zedediah shook his head. "Could've fooled me. Archie took that reporter kid down to the old highway bridge to do a little fishing."

"Fishing?" E.D. couldn't remember any member of her family ever going fishing.

"He bought a pole while he was in town, and they went out so he can practice. Seems when the television people come they'll want to get some tape of us doing regular old country things. To show that when we aren't making art, we're just plain folk. It's supposed to be good for ratings."

"Oh." E.D. set the rocking chair moving.

"Easy. Easy! You rock that hard, you're going to rock the chair right over on you. What's eating at you?"

E.D. shrugged. "Nothing."

Zedediah brushed sawdust off his work apron and settled himself in another of the rocking chairs. "Right. I can see that."

"Dad's going to give Jake a part in *The Sound of Music.* A real part. With a song and everything."

"Aaahhh."

E.D. frowned at her grandfather. "What's that supposed to mean?"

"Nothing. Just aaahhh. Anything else?"

E.D. wanted to tell him about the great spangled fritillary, but she couldn't. Just thinking about how it would sound stopped her. How could she be angry about getting some help? "And then there's Jeremy Bernstein!" she said. Why had she said that? "How come he's still here?"

"Because he doesn't have a pair of quarters to rub together. He didn't have collision insurance on that old wreck of his. He can't afford to leave!"

"Somebody could buy him a bus ticket or something."

"Are you kidding? He practically worships the ground we walk on. Who among us can resist that? The kid's obsessed with art and artists. Besides, he's got a head full of projects he wants to do about us. First the TV show. That's supposed to spin off into a feature-length documentary. Then he's planning to write separate articles about each of us and sell them to different magazines. Probably an article about the Creative Academy, too. And then there's his book. It's a good deal all the way around. He gets room and board and a place to work, and we get our own personal press agent."

Zedediah rocked for a while in unison with E.D. She realized she could hear, ever so faintly, the music up at the house. She felt her hands clench into fists.

"So Randolph thinks Jake can sing, eh?" Zedediah said.

She nodded.

"I have something to tell you, and I want you to listen. Are you listening?"

E.D. nodded again.

"I said, are you listening?"

"Yes, I'm listening!"

"All right, then. You, Edith Wharton Applewhite, have talent. Very real, very important talent. Just because somebody like Jeremy Bernstein is obsessed with artists doesn't mean that artists are the most valuable people in the world. Or that art's better than everything else human beings do."

E.D. thought of her curriculum notebook. Her project charts. Her goals and Teaching Opportunities and time lines. "I know that!" She did. She knew that. He didn't have to tell her.

But right this minute it didn't make her feel one whit better.

Chapter Sixteen

Sitting in the passenger seat of the newly repaired Miata as Randolph Applewhite drove back to Wit's End from Traybridge, Jake thought back over the evening. He had gone in to the audition with Randolph. When the Miata had pulled up in front of the theater, Jake had been surprised. He'd expected it to be like a movie house, stuck in among the storefronts on one of Traybridge's main streets. But it was a whole separate brick building, surrounded by a manicured lawn. It looked something like a library, Jake had thought, except for the tall square part at the back of the building that Randolph said was the "stage house."

Columns flanked the double front door, and there was a big red-and-yellow banner over the door that said TRAYBRIDGE LITTLE THEATRE, FIFTY-SIXTH SEASON above a pair of masks, one with its mouth turned up, the other with its mouth turned down. They had walked under the banner into a big lobby with a box office on the left side and three sets of doors ahead, leading into the auditorium, which Randolph called "the house." There were a few people milling around in the lobby when they arrived, and a great many more in the house, scattered in the rows and rows of dark blue plush seats that faced the stage. A kind of tense hush came over them when Randolph walked in.

A woman in a pale blue silk suit with upswept blond hair hurried up to talk to him. "I do hope you're going to be finishing up tonight," she said. "Our people are getting a little restive, I'm afraid."

Jake didn't know what *restive* meant, but from the way people treated one another and him in particular, he figured it must mean "hostile." From eavesdropping on their conversations, Jake discovered that everybody who had ever been in a Little Theatre show, and lots of people who hadn't, wanted to get cast, or have their children cast, in a show directed by a real, professional, New York director. But auditions had been going on too long, with no sign of when Randolph would announce the cast. There was considerable tension in the air. He heard any number of whispered references to his hair and his eyebrow ring. He wasn't the only target. Thinly veiled insults were whispered about a whole lot of other people, too, as they sang or read scenes.

When it had been Jake's turn to get up onstage, he had sung "Sixteen Going on Seventeen" with Jeannie Ng, learned a few dance steps from the odd little man who was doing the choreography, danced with Jeannie Ng, and then read Rolf's big scene—with Jeannie Ng. Jeannie was small and slim, with long black hair, and dark, almond-shaped eyes in a serenely beautiful face. Her singing voice was sensational. Nervous as he'd been, she had such a calm presence that just being onstage with her somehow made him think he could do it. And he could! He had. Even Jake knew he'd been good.

Another boy, a red-haired and freckled boy who really was seventeen-going-on-eighteen, had also sung and danced and read the part of Rolf, not with Jeannie, but with a blond girl who, when she wasn't auditioning, kept finding ways to mention various other parts she had played in Traybridge Little Theatre productions—the first of which, she said four or five times, had been when she was only five years old. Jake knew absolutely nothing about theater, but he knew that the blond girl, however many parts she had played, and however early she had started playing them, couldn't hold a candle to Jeannie Ng. And the red-haired boy, who seemed to be a pretty good actor, couldn't sing at all.

Jake had just managed to finish reading the play before they left for the audition. He didn't think it was as bad as Randolph had said. It was about a family of Austrians—the von Trapps—at the beginning of the Second World War, when Germany occupied Austria. The Baron von Trapp, an Austrian naval officer whose wife had died, hired a young woman from a nearby convent to be a governess to his seven children. After the governess had taught all the children to sing, the baron fell in love with her. When the Nazis invaded Austria, they demanded that the baron join the German navy. Instead, the whole family, including the governess who had by that time become his wife, used their singing at a music festival as a cover to escape over the mountains into Switzerland.

Rolf, the part Jake had read for, was a messenger boy who was in love with the oldest von Trapp daughter. By the end of the play he had joined the SS, which was the Nazi security force, and was helping the Germans look for the von Trapps to keep them from escaping. It was Rolf who, because of his love for Liesl, let the family get away.

"So," Randolph said now as they turned into the

driveway at Wit's End. "It'll be you and Jeannie doing Rolf and Liesl. You're not a bad actor. And you can dance as much as you'll need to. Plus, you're just tall enough and she's just small enough that you'll look okay together onstage. The Ngs are a talented family. I'm going to use her younger brother to play Kurt. What is that ungodly sound?"

A wail that reminded Jake of a tornado siren gave way suddenly to deep barking. As they curved around the trees and shrubs, the Miata's headlights picked up an astonishing sight. Winston, tail waving, ears flapping, barking frantically, came running—galloping—toward them from the house. When Randolph stopped the car, the dog threw himself at it, leaping at the passenger door, whining and barking. "Keep that bloody beast's claws off my car!" Randolph shouted as Jake opened his door. "What do you suppose is the matter with him?"

With an ungainly leap, Winston managed to launch himself from the driveway onto Jake's lap, landing like a ten-ton truck, his back claws digging into Jake's legs, his tongue slathering Jake's face with foamy saliva.

Right behind him came Cordelia and Sybil. "What have you done to that dog, Jake Semple?" Cordelia was asking as she came, her voice accusing. "He's gone completely berserk!"

"I—I—" Jake couldn't have said more even if he'd

had anything more to say. He had to close his mouth firmly against the onslaught of basset greeting.

"He started to howl when the two of you drove away," Sybil said, "and he hasn't stopped for fifteen seconds since. It's been *hours*! He has sat on the front porch and howled as if the world were coming to an end." She waved her reading glasses in the air. Jake had the feeling that she would have preferred to beat him with them. "I can't think, much less work, with that racket going on. If it isn't *The Sound of Music,* it's the wretched hound. I might as well give up writing altogether."

"You can't go away anymore," Cordelia said to Jake. "That's all there is to it. Not without Winston. Nothing would make him stop. I offered him liver treats, his favorite, and he looked at me as if I was out of my mind. He was inconsolable. Wherever you go, you have to take Winston with you!"

"What are you two going on about? Jake's going to be at rehearsals every night. I can't have a dog at rehearsals," Randolph said. "Under no circumstances will I have a dog at my rehearsals!"

"Then you can't have Jake either," Sybil said. "Your choice. If you want Jake in your show, you're going to have to have Winston. I will not have him here howling like a soul in torment. That's all there is to it."

"But what if he starts howling at rehearsal?"

"He won't." E.D. had joined them. "Not if Jake's

there," she said. "He's gotten it into his doggy brain that he's Jake's dog and that's all there is to it." She frowned at Jake. "*Alienation of affections* it's called, and people can get sued for it."

"Not when it's a *dog*," Cordelia said.

"Yeah, well, Winston's *our* dog, and now he thinks he's Jake's dog."

Jake had finally succeeded in dislodging Winston from his lap. The dog was now sitting on the drive, staring up at him and wagging his tail so hard that his whole body wagged with it. "I didn't do anything! I just feed him a little and pet him once in a while. Nobody else seems to take any notice of him at all."

"I do!" E.D. said. "At least I used to, before he turned into your shadow. Now he won't so much as look at me. Or anybody else except you."

"Not even with liver treats!" Cordelia said.

"Enough, enough, enough!" Randolph said. "We will deal with the question of the dog some other time. Let's go inside. I'm calling a family meeting. Right now."

"A family meeting? Everybody?" E.D. said.

"Everybody except Destiny. And Hal. I haven't lost touch with reality."

Sybil checked her watch. "It's nearly eleven o'clock! Lucille and Archie will be asleep by now."

"Well, then, wake them up! Send that howling monster of a dog over to roust them out. We need a family celebration! And someone get that Bernstein fellow up here. This involves him, too, if he really intends to do that documentary he's talking about. I have news. Wonderful news. I have finally succeeded in casting the show!"

Chapter Seventeen

"You're kidding!" Sybil had just brought in a tray of coffee, and she set it down with a bang so that coffee sloshed out of the mugs.

E.D. thought it was unlikely that her father had dragged everybody to a meeting to make a joke. Zedediah hadn't come—he'd told her when she went to get him that unless someone was at death's door at that very moment, he saw no reason why whatever it was couldn't perfectly well wait until morning. But Lucille and Archie were there, even though she'd had to wake them. They were sitting blearily on the couch in their nightclothes. Jeremy Bernstein was there, too, complete with notebook and pen.

"Why would I kid about a thing like this? It's been the most grueling audition process I've ever been through in my life. And the hardest part of it was finding the person to play Maria. Annalouise Mabry sings *and* acts, and she's young and pretty besides. She is absolutely perfect for the part!"

"Well, it will certainly get the show some attention," Sybil said. "I don't know that anyone has ever cast an African American as Maria before."

"That's because nobody else had to cast the show in Traybridge, North Carolina, before."

"I thought *The Sound of Music* was a true story," E.D. said. "Wasn't Maria von Trapp a real person?"

"Of course," her father said. "The guiding force behind the von Trapp Family Singers."

"But she wasn't black."

Jeremy Bernstein took a cup of coffee off the tray and blotted its bottom with a napkin. "Technically speaking, the show is only *based* on a true story. It's literature—a piece of musical theater—not a documentary. Rodgers and Hammerstein probably took some liberties with the truth in creating it. Your father can take a few when casting it. It's called *color-blind casting*." He turned to Randolph. "That's what makes you such an extraordinary director! That you have the courage, the vision, to make such a choice."

"It was the only possible choice," Randolph said. "Annalouise is incredibly talented. She graduated from Northwestern with a degree in musical theater. She's the lead singer in a gospel choir that's toured the country three times. If I hadn't located this girl, I'd have had to call the whole project off. There wasn't a single other possible Maria for a hundred miles in any direction. She isn't the only color-blind choice, though. It's going to be a rainbow cast. The children playing Louisa and Friedrich are black, and Liesl and Kurt are Vietnamese."

"Wait a minute, wait a minute," E.D. said. "I get it that the show isn't a documentary. But won't the audience have trouble understanding it? The von Trapp children all have the same parents. There's biology to think about. You can't have three different races in one family! It doesn't make sense."

"It makes perfect sense! It's musical theater. Singing. Acting. A little dancing. The kids I cast sing and act better than anyone else in town."

"Color-blind casting is the *right* thing to do," Jeremy said. "Biology or not, your father's morally bound to cast the best people regardless of color or ethnic background."

"Exactly!" Randolph said, stirring a heaping spoonful of sugar into his coffee. "Anyway, appearances don't count. Once the show gets started, I guarantee that the audience won't notice."

Sybil shook her head. "Well, they're likely to *notice*."

Jeremy waved his coffee mug in the air. "I think it's a philosophically powerful concept. What's *The Sound of Music* about, after all?"

"Falling in love and escaping the Nazis," Cordelia said.

Jeremy nodded. "Escaping the Nazis. What were the Nazis most infamous for? The Holocaust—the killing of six million Jews. One of the most terrible examples of racial hatred in modern times. What better way to hold a mirror up to our own prejudices than to cast this particular show across racial lines. It's positively *inspired*!" He began jotting in his notebook. "Think of it. Probably the first time *The Sound of Music* has ever been done this way. And it's being done in the South. This'll make a great hook for the TV show. The network people will love it. We can have them come for the opening."

Randolph grinned. "That's it, of course. I cast the show the way I did for philosophical reasons."

That was an outrageous lie, E.D. thought, and everyone in the room knew it. But from now on, she knew, that was how her father would think about it. And that's the way Jeremy would write about it.

"I told you I would give the show an edge, Cordelia. Didn't I? Didn't I? I said I would send the audience away both humming and thinking."

"Let's hope the Little Theatre board doesn't pull the plug on you and cancel the whole thing," Sybil said. "Traybridge might not be quite ready for this."

"They wouldn't dare!"

Lucille stifled a yawn. "I think it's wonderful that you finally got your cast, Randolph. I'm sure it will all work out. Never fear, Sybil, there's a shift in consciousness happening these days all over the world. Unity out of diversity. It's surely happening in Traybridge, too. There's nothing to worry about."

In Lucille's view of the world, E.D. thought, there was *never* anything to worry about. She looked over at Jake, who was sitting at the end of the couch with Winston draped across his feet. He was staring into space as if he hadn't heard a word that was being said. There was an odd look in his eyes. It reminded her, somehow, of the look Cordelia got when she started talking about her ballet.

"We need to be getting back to bed," Lucille said then. She nudged Archie, who had fallen asleep where he sat. "Let's go. Govindaswami will be here bright and early."

"Who?" Randolph asked. "Who'll be here?"

"Ravi Govindaswami. My guru. Don't tell me you've forgotten that, too! He's going to be staying in Sweet Gum Cottage."

"Your guru's coming to stay? Tomorrow?" Sybil asked in a horrified voice. "Why didn't you warn us?"

Lucille stood, pulling at Archie's arm. "I did warn you. Nobody pays attention to anything around here except their own projects."

"But I haven't had time to do the grocery shopping yet this week. We won't have enough food—again!"

"That's all right. Govindaswami is fasting."

As E.D. slipped into sleep later, she was glad she didn't have anything to do with her father's show. She was beginning to have a strong premonition of catastrophe.

Chapter Eighteen

Jake had finished gelling his hair. Now he turned his face one way and then another so that the light above the mirror picked up the dusting of hair on his upper lip. Darken that down and he could pass for seventeen—couldn't he? Not according to the red-haired kid who'd expected to get cast as Rolf and ended up playing an anonymous soldier instead. "It's ridiculous for you to play that part. No way an audience is going to believe you're old enough to get into the SS." What the red-haired kid thought didn't count, Jake reminded himself. Or what anybody else in the show thought either, for that matter. About anything.

Last night they'd had their first rehearsal, and Randolph had made that very clear at the beginning. The director, he had told the assembled cast, made the decisions, starting with casting, and anybody who didn't like those decisions could go do another show somewhere else for some other director. He had directed in theaters all over the country and had had a smash Off-Broadway hit, and he intended to maintain a professional atmosphere at all times. "I am a professional and I will expect every one of you to behave as if you are, too. I don't put up with lateness, laziness, or sloppy work. You will not be called to every rehearsal, but when you are called, you will arrive on time and you will be prepared. When you are not actually onstage, you will be silent and respectful of the actors who *are* onstage. There is no place in a Randolph Applewhite production for amateurs who behave like amateurs."

If he hadn't started that way, Jake thought, there might have been open rebellion. There had been so much hostility in the air when they first came in that Winston had gone right underneath a folding chair in the corner and hadn't come out again until it was time to go home.

Nobody except the leads had been happy with the casting. The people who'd *expected* to get the leads were playing unnamed townspeople or nuns or storm troopers instead. There were so many people in the show that, except for the children, Randolph had had to cast almost everyone who had auditioned. But it hadn't made them happy. "I've been with the Little Theatre since the building was the Masonic fellowship hall," he'd heard one man say, "and I've never played *anything* but a major role! Now he's brought in all these—these—outsiders and given them the plum parts. It's a travesty!"

"There are no small parts," the woman he was talking to said. "Only small—"

"Easy for you to say. You have *lines*!"

"Little Priscilla Montrose didn't even get cast," someone else said. "The daughter of the president of the board!"

"And *she* actually looks the part!"

After Randolph's speech about professionalism, people quit complaining, but the atmosphere hadn't really changed till rehearsal was over and he mentioned the possibility that a TV crew would tape some of their work for national television. "And why, you ask, do they wish to focus on the Traybridge Little Theatre?" Randolph asked. "Because we are doing something different, something important—an edgy, innovative, truly American version of a classic of the musical theater." Jake didn't know whether anyone bought the philosophy part, but the prospect of being on national television had settled them right down.

Now Winston, who had been whining at the bathroom door, began to scratch to come in. Jake sighed. He opened the door and Winston waddled in, his tail wagging furiously. "Hey, old guy—you don't care whether I look thirteen or seventeen, do you?" he asked, rubbing Winston's ears. The dog's long tongue swiped across his hand, leaving a trail of saliva. Jake wiped it off on his pants. "Disgusting," he told the dog as he patted his head. "That's what you are, disgusting."

An hour later, when the family gathered for breakfast at the main house, Lucille's guru joined them. Jake had seen him coming up toward the house from the cottage he was staying in and couldn't get over the idea that the man was a sort of human version of Winston. He was short and round, dressed in voluminous pants and a long tunic, and moved as he walked the way the dog did, almost as much from side to side as straight ahead. He had the same dark, solemn, almost mournful eyes. In Winston these were contradicted by a perpetually wagging tail, in Govindaswami by a perpetually sunny smile. "I am having a cup of tea," he told them, beaming as he settled himself into the chair at the head of the table, "so as to join with you for the fellowship. I hope you will not be offended by my fast."

Far from being offended, Jake thought, the family

was thrilled not to have to share their breakfast. Jeremy Bernstein offered, as he stared at the single spoonful of scrambled eggs that was left in the bowl when it had been passed to him, to take the grocery list to Traybridge. Archie agreed to lend him his pickup.

After breakfast Jake slipped into the schoolroom, took an empty coffee can and a printout he'd made from the Internet, and hurried around to Lucille's vegetable garden. Lucille had come in that morning just as he and Winston emerged from the bathroom, complaining loudly that there were caterpillars all over her parsley, eating it down to the stems.

She had asked them kindly to leave, and they hadn't gone, she said. That method had worked with slugs and earwigs and even aphids. But the caterpillars had refused to listen to her. She wouldn't use poison and didn't even like to pick them off, because whatever caterpillars started eating they had to go on eating, or they'd starve. She'd consulted with the nature spirits, and they had had no advice except to relinquish her need for control. "So I guess we'll just have to leave the parsley to the caterpillars and do without. So much for the tabouli I was planning to make."

"You can put parsley on the grocery list and get it from the grocery," Archie had suggested.

"Oh, sure! Covered with pesticides and probably

genetically altered besides."

Lucille's complaints had given Jake an idea. In the garden he found exactly what he'd been hoping to find. As Lucille had said, the parsley was covered with green-and-black-striped caterpillars that were busy eating all the leaves. Stem after stem had its caterpillar, some small and newly hatched, others fat and almost ready to pupate. He checked them against the photograph on the printout. Just as he'd thought, they were the larval stage of one of the most beautiful of the Carolina butterflies, the black swallowtail. Black swallowtails had a particular preference for parsley, the printout said. Carefully, he picked the caterpillars off the parsley plants and put them into the coffee can. Then he picked the rest of the leaves off the parsley plants and put them in with the caterpillars. It wasn't enough to feed them for long. He would add parsley to the grocery list before Bernstein went to town. He hoped if he washed it carefully, the store parsley wouldn't hurt the caterpillars. Back in the schoolroom, he found an empty aquarium that would be just perfect for his plan.

Today was Zedediah's day to be teacher on call. Unlike the rest of the family, Zedediah had a habit of actually showing up. He'd even demand to see what they'd been doing and ask them questions about it. Jake hated Zedediah's days. On his first one the old man had asked Jake what gave him joy. Jake hadn't understood the question. "You mean what do I like to do?"

"I mean," Zedediah had said, "exactly what I said. *What gives you joy?*"

Jake hadn't been able to come up with an answer.

"Once you know that, you will know what you want from an education and you'll be able to set your own program. Meantime, just do what E.D. is doing." Every time Zedediah had been on call since then, when he checked out whatever work Jake had done, he'd given him a look that seemed to say that Jake Semple was a screwup who was never going to amount to anything. E.D., of course, never got such a look.

At least he'd have something to show Zedediah this time. Not something E.D. had thought up. He put the caterpillars and the parsley into the aquarium and added a couple of sticks, propped against the glass and held in place with lumps of modeling clay. Then he tied a piece of cheesecloth over the top of the aquarium to keep the caterpillars in and lettered a sign that said METAMORPHOSIS, A LIVING DEMONSTRATION. He taped the sign to the front of the aquarium. This would be an infinitely better Teaching Opportunity than a papier-mâché caterpillar and chrysalis. Destiny—and all the rest of the family, for that matter—would get to watch the caterpillars pupate and then turn into butterflies.

The Internet website that had had the photo of the

black swallowtail caterpillar had advised keeping butterflies inside once they'd emerged from their pupa state rather than releasing them. That way they could be cared for and guarded all the way through the life cycle. More butterflies could be safely raised indoors that way and eventually released to increase their numbers in the wild. Butterflies were in trouble, it said, from pesticides and habitat loss. Raising them for release could help. The website gave a recipe for feeding the butterflies once they hatched. They would get to know you and come land on your hand to feed, it said. You could offer the concoction, made of soy sauce, Gatorade, and milk, and they would unroll their long, strawlike tongues and suck it up. The mixture sounded disgusting, but the website promised that the butterflies would love it. You could also make a plain sugar syrup or just put out a piece of ripe melon where they could get to it, and they would feed themselves.

He draped newspapers over the aquarium so E.D. and Zedediah wouldn't see it the minute they came in, and then sat down at his desk with a book about the Civil War E.D had given him. When E.D. came in and began gathering what she had done during the week to show Zedediah, Jake began humming the title song from *The Sound of Music*. Before she had a chance to react, Zedediah arrived with Destiny, who was loudly yodeling the song about the lonely goatherd. As usual, he was slightly off-key.

"Zedediah," E.D. said, "make him stop!"

"That's enough now," Zedediah said to Destiny.

"What's a goatherd?" Destiny asked.

"A boy who takes the goats up to the pastures in the mountains to feed. And watches out for them. Protects them."

"And why is he lonely?"

"You'd be lonely, too, if your only friends were goats," E.D. said as she held out her curriculum notebook to Zedediah. "I've checked off everything I've finished. My report on the Battle of Gettysburg is all done—I just haven't had a chance to print it out yet. Jeremy's been on the computer a lot."

"We must let him know that you need your time on it, too. Maybe Hal can let him use his sometimes." Zedediah looked over E.D.'s notebook. "Good. Good. I see you've started reading *A Midsummer Night's Dream*." He turned to Jake. "Have you begun it yet?"

Jake shook his head. "I'm reading *Hamlet* instead. Because of Cordelia's ballet." He could tell by the look on her face that E.D. hadn't read *Hamlet* yet. Good. He'd actually be ahead of her on something then.

"How far have you gotten in it?"

"Not that far. It's slow going. I've been taking it with me to rehearsals, but it's hard to concentrate there."

"I hope you aren't going to let your role in *The Sound of Music* interfere with your schoolwork. We have an obligation to your grandfather to be sure you do a little learning while you're here, you know."

Zedediah was giving him that look again. Was he warning Jake that the show could get snatched away from him like a cigarette or his headphones? "We only have rehearsals at night," Jake said. "I can read it during the day."

"Good."

"I've finished the Butterfly Project, though," Jake said.

"You can't have!" E.D. protested. "It was already done."

Jake went to the aquarium and whisked away the newspapers. "This is a different way—a better way—to do the Teaching Opportunity. Destiny can see the whole process of metamorphosis—in real life."

E.D. stared into the aquarium. "What are those?" She looked more carefully. "Black swallowtails?"

Jake nodded, humming "The Lonely Goatherd" quietly to himself.

"Are those worm thingies going to gets to be butterflies?" Destiny asked. Jake nodded again. "And do I gets to see them grow their wings?"

"Absolutely."

"Yay, Jake!"

Jake smiled at E.D., who glowered back at him. Score one for the delinquent kid.

Chapter Nineteen

For a week Govindaswami had been teaching them to meditate. E.D. had put meditation under Healthful Living in her curriculum notebook so that she could count it as an academic accomplishment. She was sitting cross-legged on the schoolroom floor now, concentrating on her breathing. In. Out. In. Out. It was supposed to keep her from thinking. Center her. Calm her. Right now it didn't seem to be working. What she wanted to do was scream.

Hal had refused to let Jeremy Bernstein use his

computer. When Sybil had broached the subject, speaking to Hal's closed door, he had said that he was creating a website where he could sell his sculpture and he needed his computer every minute. Besides, he couldn't let anyone into his room any more than he could come out of his room himself. "I need my creative privacy," he had shouted through the door. So Jeremy had been allowed to take over the schoolroom computer almost completely.

He was at the keyboard now, tapping away. He'd been there last night when she'd finally given up and gone to bed. This morning he had been there already at eight-thirty. She'd been trying to read *A Midsummer Night's Dream* while she waited for him to finish whatever it was he was doing now, but the incessant tap of the computer keys had made it impossible to concentrate. She hadn't done her math. She hadn't written the story she was supposed to write for language arts.

She'd gone to her father about it as soon as he got up, to beg him to put his foot down either with Hal or with Jeremy. But he'd told her that things were going badly with the Traybridge Little Theatre. He had a meeting with the technical staff that afternoon to sort things out, and he had no psychic energy left over for trivialities. *Trivialities!*

She'd taken the problem to her mother then. That had been a mistake. She had stuck her head into her mother's office and her mother had thrown a dictionary at her. Well, maybe not actually *at* her. It had missed by a foot. Sybil Jameson was having writer's block. E.D. wished her mother had told the family that. She never would have gone near the office if she'd known. They all knew better than to go near Sybil during a block.

That was Jeremy's fault, too, E.D. thought. With him there doing his article about Sybil's Great American Novel, asking her questions about it, begging to be allowed to read the newest bits of it, she didn't dare to admit that the Great American Novel had come to a screeching halt. "Plot!" she had told E.D. after apologizing for throwing the dictionary. "That's the whole trouble. I keep writing *plot*. I actually killed a character off yesterday morning. I couldn't help myself. My masterpiece is turning inexorably into a Petunia Grantham mystery!" E.D. had ended up going down to the kitchen to make her mother a soothing cup of tea.

She'd tried to find Archie then, but he'd gone fishing. Archie had become unaccountably obsessed with fishing. Lucille, who had been meditating herself when E.D. found her, looked up at her and smiled through a wreath of incense. The smile reminded E.D. of Govindaswami's. "What can possibly be wrong in the present moment?" Lucille had said to her. "Ask yourself that and you'll find the answer." E.D. had no idea what that meant, but she could recognize a dead end when she encountered it.

Even Zedediah had let her down. "Consider it an unexpected blessing," he'd said. "You don't want to sit at a computer now. It's October. The leaves are turning. The air is cooling off. Day after day we have sunshine and blue sky. But it's all too fleeting. The rainy season's on its way. Go out now, while the world is still perfect. Smell it. Listen to it. Take it in before it goes."

"I thought you wanted us to *learn*!" she'd said.

"There are many ways to learn," her grandfather had said.

E.D. discovered, now, that she had lost track of her breathing altogether. *In. Out.* It was no good. She opened her eyes—and saw immediately Jake's metamorphosis project. Almost half of the caterpillars were now dark curved shapes hanging by thin threads from the twigs he'd put in. The others were busily munching away on bunches of parsley, growing ever fatter, leaving piles of tiny dark green balls of caterpillar dung on the floor of the aquarium. She hated Jake Semple. Of course this was a better idea than papier-mâché. Why had it never occurred to *her* to collect caterpillars?

The day Jake had made the aquarium had been the last day he and E.D. had been a class. It had been agreed at dinner that night that there wasn't really any more need for clumping them. Jake had shown initiative. Good sense. Creativity. Even cooperation. So Jake could do his thing, whatever, besides singing, he decided that thing might be, and she could go back to doing hers.

Since then, as far as she could tell, Jake's thing had had almost nothing to do with real work. His thing had been to go hiking with Winston. Most of the time Destiny tagged along. They'd take lunch in a backpack and come back late in the afternoon, sweaty or muddy, singing at the top of their lungs. Then they'd check to see if any butterflies had hatched and unload whatever they'd collected on their rambles. Jake called it all natural history. E.D. called it clutter.

The schoolroom was littered with their mess. There were shoe boxes full of bright leaves, bowls full of hickory and beechnuts, pinecones and acorns; there were bird feathers, stones, and a big jar of slimy green water from the pond that Destiny claimed was full of "teensy buggy things" that they would check on every so often with a big magnifying glass. Jake hadn't even looked for a book that would tell them what the buggy things were! Destiny called everything they brought back, just like the caterpillars, "magics." Her little brother might learn about metamorphosis, but it seemed perfectly clear to E.D. that he was learning nothing else at all.

She disentangled her legs and got up from the floor. If she couldn't write or do her math or do research on the Internet, she'd take her copy of *A Midsummer Night's Dream* outside and finish reading it before the rainy season.

She had just gotten it out of her desk when she heard a car skid to a stop on the driveway, and a car door slam, followed by footsteps thundering up onto the porch. "Help!" The front door banged open and then slammed shut. *"Help!"* It was her father's voice, booming so that he could have been heard halfway to Traybridge. *"Help,* I said. *Help! Help! Help!* Where is this family when you need them?" There was a pause. Then, *"FIRE!"*

Jeremy leaped up from his seat at the computer. He and E.D. collided as they tried to get through the schoolroom door at the same time. When they got to the front hall, Sybil was coming down the stairs, her hair disheveled, her computer glasses bouncing on her chest. Cordelia came from the kitchen, a doughnut in her hand.

"They're right," her father said. "Never yell for help these days. Nobody wants to help. But yell 'Fire' and they come like bats out of hell, intent on saving their own skins."

"What is it?" Sybil asked. "What's happened?"

By this time Lucille and Govindaswami and Zedediah had all reached the front porch and were trying unsucessfully to sort out who would hold the door and who would come in through it. "Is someone dying?" Govindaswami asked. "Take me to him. Who is it?"

"Not who—what," Randolph said. *"Dying! Dead!"*

"There's no need to yell anymore," Sybil said. "We're all here now. At least everybody within a radius of five miles is here. What are you talking about?"

"My show! I'm talking about my show. *The Sound of Music.* You may have heard of it."

"No need for sarcasm, Randolph," Zedediah said.

"They've all quit!"

"Who's all quit?" Cordelia asked.

"The entire technical staff. Designer, costumer, choreographer, lights, props, *even the stage manager*! Murder, that's what it is. Cold-blooded murder."

"What happened?"

"What happened? I just told you. They all quit. I called a technical meeting to sort out a few problems, and ten minutes into it they all just got up and walked out. No reason whatsoever!"

"There must have been a reason. People don't just—"

"That wretched Montrose woman put them up to it, that's the reason. Ever since I refused to cast that untalented little brat of hers, she's been looking for a way to get rid of me. But she couldn't just cancel the show, not with the way I cast it. Someone might think it was racism. The theater might lose its funding."

"But what did they *say* the reason was?" Sybil persisted.

"Oh, well. They *said* that I was too demanding. They *said* I was a perfectionist. That I didn't respect them—the stupid, incompetent, clueless ignoramuses. Now I ask you—"

"Sounds about right to me," Zedediah said.

"Don't start, Father."

"Oh," Sybil said. "Oh, I get it now. I understand why you came in hollering 'Help!' at the top of your lungs. You've gone and bullied those poor people—"

"Bullied? Bullied? I'm the director. They're the tech staff—"

"—you've gone and bullied and belittled those poor people until they couldn't take it anymore, and now you expect us to come running to the rescue."

"I expect my talented and creative family to gather around me and support me in my hour of need."

"Nobody asked you to accept that job, Randolph."

"It's my work! I'm a director. I direct. They offered me a show and I took it on. Which of you would have done anything different? This is a crisis. An emergency. A screaming disaster."

"The rest of us have our work, too," Sybil said.

Lucille put her hand on Randolph's arm. "What, exactly, do you need?"

"Costumes. Sets. Props. Choreography. Music. Lights. Everything!"

"I can do costumes," Lucille said. She turned to Sybil. "We could do them together. You could use a little break from the Great American Novel, couldn't you?"

Sybil stood for a moment, her hand on the stair railing. She glanced at Jeremy Bernstein and then looked back at Lucille, carefully avoiding E.D.'s eyes. "Well—it would be a great sacrifice, of course. The book has been going so smoothly. But—all right." She turned to Randolph. "I'll do it on one condition."

Randolph sighed loudly. "What condition is that?"

"That you don't try bullying *me*. If your family is going to save your skin, you'd better remember that we're all artists in our own right. You may direct. You may not bully!"

"You know me, my dear. I always give respect where respect is due."

The door at the top of the stairs opened a crack. "I'll design the set," Hal's voice called down. The door clicked shut again.

"I suppose Archie and I could build it," Zedediah said.

"All right, all right," Cordelia said. She took a bite of the doughnut. "I'll do the choreography."

"I need someone to play the music," Randolph said. "Could you play the show, too?"

Cordelia shook her head. "I don't read music. You know that. I play by ear."

"I could contribute," Govindaswami said. "I could play the music on my sitar."

"Sitar? That Indian stringed instrument? Ah—ah, well—thank you. It's good of you to offer. But I don't think Rodgers and Hammerstein thought of having the score orchestrated for sitar."

Jeremy Bernstein cleared his throat. "Er . . . um. Excuse me, but perhaps I could play the show."

"Wonderful!" Randolph said. "The theater has a halfway decent synthesizer. I can arrange for you to—"

"Um. I have never actually played a synthesizer."

"What do you play? A dulcimer, I suppose. Or a didgeridoo."

There was a long silence. Finally Jeremy mumbled something that E.D. couldn't hear. Her father hadn't heard either.

"What? What do you play?"

Bernstein cleared his throat again and said, "The accordion."

"You're kidding."

Bernstein looked up, his mouth tightening. "I am not kidding! I learned during my family's summers in the Poconos when I was a kid. I wore a satin shirt and played in an accordion band!"

"You have your accordion with you?"

He shook his head. "Of course not. Nobody knows. I haven't told a soul about this since I left junior high school. But I could have my mother ship it."

"Accordion. *The Sound of Music* on the accordion. Well, why not?" Randolph said. "It's better than kazoos."

E.D. turned and headed back toward the schoolroom. As intense and dramatic as all this was, it had nothing to do with her. Her father needed everybody else, not her.

"E.D.!" her father called. "Where are you going?"

"To get my Shakespeare," she said. "You don't need me."

"Don't need you? Didn't you hear me say my stage manager quit? Of course I need you—more than anyone. There's nobody else in this family even remotely organized enough to handle the job! There's no time for Shakespeare now! There's work to be done."

E.D. gave her head a little shake as if to clear her ears. Her father dug into his briefcase and came up with a fat spiral notebook, a yellow legal pad covered with handwritten notes, and a calendar. He held them out to her. "Let's go someplace where we won't be disturbed. I need you all caught up and ready to go before tonight's rehearsal. I'll talk to the rest of you at dinner."

Chapter Twenty

Jake was trying to get ready for rehearsal with Destiny, yodeling the lonely goatherd song in his wake, when it dawned on him that his life had slipped finally and utterly out of his control.

He'd become impossibly entangled with the Applewhites. First Winston had adopted him and then, by what seemed the same invisible and mysterious process, Destiny had, too. The kid had begun explaining to anyone who would listen that Jake was the "bestest brother in the whole wide world." Jake had told him and told him that just because he had come to live at Wit's End it didn't mean he was Destiny's brother, but Destiny was impervious to minor details of fact.

When the family took over all the technical jobs on *The Sound of Music,* everybody was too busy working on the show to have time to look after a four-year-old. Jake only had to go to rehearsal. He had more time than anybody. And since Destiny had already adopted him anyway, he had somehow become a kind of full-time baby-sitter. Nobody had actually *asked* him to look after Destiny, and he hadn't exactly volunteered. It had just happened.

Jake could understand why Hal wasn't enough of a brother for Destiny. The set designs had appeared outside his door as he finished them. Then he'd built a model, which had also been left in the hall during the night, followed by the renderings—the drawings that Zedediah and Archie were using to build the parts of the set they could build in the wood shop. So far none of this had required Hal to come out of his room. Jake had still never met him face-to-face.

Wit's End had become a beehive of theatrical activity. The number of costumes required was vastly greater than Lucille and Sybil could handle alone, so Cordelia, who had quickly finished the choreography and only had to go to a few rehearsals, was immediately drafted into the costume crew. Lucille had a sewing machine, but two more had been rented and bolts and bolts of cloth brought from town. When even the three of them, working steadily and grumbling loudly, could not churn out nuns' habits fast enough, they shanghaied Govindaswami, who was pretty good with a needle, to help.

Jake had no idea what a guru normally did, except for meditating, which didn't seem to be a full-time occupation. But if Govindaswami was any sort of example, gurus had a variety of talents. After Randolph's emergency had been declared, when it became clear that nobody had time to fix meals, Govindaswami had abandoned his fast and taken over the kitchen. His sewing was adequate, but his cooking turned out to be spectacular. Dramatic, intense—*hot*—but spectacular.

Grocery runs were no longer a haphazard occurrence. Having quickly discovered that Traybridge had no grocery that stocked the ingredients he needed, Govindaswami would borrow Archie's pickup and disappear for hours at a time, coming back with huge bags of rice, bags and boxes of meats and vegetables, and various strange herbs and spices, from which he concocted meals the like of which Jake had never encountered. Once, after Wolfie had gotten loose again and torn open a huge burlap bag full of rice that Govindaswami had set on the ground by the truck while he took the rest of his purchases inside, Jake had seen the man looking speculatively at the goat.

But Jake figured that had been only his imagination. Even if Indians ate goat, which Jake didn't think they did, Govindaswami would never go after Lucille's beloved Wolfie.

It was an education in itself to watch Govindaswami in the kitchen. "Passion," he would say to Jake and Destiny as he moved around the room, chopping and stirring and tasting. "Passion is necessary to all of life. All of life. Meditating, working, cooking, eating. Especially eating!"

It took the Applewhites no time at all to adapt to the change in their dietary habits. Cordelia even gave up her green gunk. No matter how busy they were, everybody stopped whatever they were doing at lunch, and again at dinnertime, to gather in the dining room for the feasts Govindaswami prepared. There were curries, chutneys, and wonderful soft flatbreads. As much food as appeared on the table invariably disappeared before the end of the meal. Some of the dishes were so spicy they were almost too painful to eat, but Govindaswami explained that yogurt and sugar both cooled the tongue. He served plenty of yogurt sauces and gallons of Destiny's favorite, grape Kool-Aid.

It was such a dinner they had just finished. Jake's mouth still tingled from the lamb curry. Now he was doing his best to make sure he had everything he would need at rehearsal. It wasn't easy. The other actors only had to take their script, maybe a bottle of water, and something to do while they were waiting to go onstage. Jake had to take Winston's leash, in case the dog needed to go out during rehearsal, his water dish, and a bag of liver treats to distract him from howling along with the accordion. There was something about certain notes on the accordion that sent the dog into long, drawn-out howls that only liver treats could stop. Winston's essential items were already packed in one of the large canvas bags Lucille had provided.

Destiny's needs were considerably more complicated. It wasn't easy to keep the kid busy and occupied and out of mischief for the three or four, sometimes even five hours of rehearsal. Even for a four-year-old, Destiny's boredom threshhold seemed extraordinarily low. Every night Jake filled the bags with as many distractions as he could think of. He took picture books—never the same ones twice in a row. He took a thick pad of paper and watercolor markers. And he always threw in a few toys, though Destiny did not seem particularly interested in toys.

During the last rehearsal, Destiny had found a screwdriver somewhere and spent the whole time Jake was onstage unscrewing seat bottoms in the auditorium. No one had noticed what he was doing until Mrs. Montrose, who had come to observe the rehearsal, sat down in one of the unscrewed seats. It detached and crashed to the floor, taking her with it. She had blamed Randolph. Randolph had blamed Jake.

So now Jake scoured the schoolroom to come up with new ideas. He added a few handfuls of Legos, some brightly colored sticks of modeling clay, and a box full of miniature cars. "Anything else you want to take?" he asked Destiny.

Destiny stopped singing to ponder this question. "The caterpillars," he said.

"Can't take the caterpillars," Jake told him.

"What if they gets to be butterflies while we're gone?"

"They won't all do it at the same time," Jake assured him. "I'll take off the top, and if one does, it'll be here fluttering around the schoolroom when we get back."

Destiny went back to his song. Cordelia hurried in, carrying a pair of dark brown pants and a shirt. She tossed them at Jake. "Your messenger uniform. At least I think it'll do. I don't know what messengers wore in Austria in the thirties. But take it with you and wear it for your scene tonight. See what the Emperor of the World thinks. If he likes it, I can scratch another costume off the list. Except for the hat. We don't have a hat yet."

Destiny stopped singing. "I want a uniform! Make me one too, Delia! With a hat."

"It's a costume. You're not in the show. You don't get

a costume." Cordelia's voice was tight.

"But I want one! Like Jake's. With a hat. I wanna—"

"Listen, you little beast, there are forty-six people in this show and most of them have at least four costumes! *You do not get a costume!*"

"I only have two," Jake said. "This one and the SS uniform. Randolph said those are rented."

"Yeah. But we have to do alterations to make them fit. I am not a costumer. I am a dancer! A choreographer! Never again, I tell you. Never, ever, ever again!" Cordelia turned to go. "Thank heavens for the Mother Abbess," she muttered as she left. "One habit for the whole show. And I've finished it."

Jake folded the uniform and put it into the bag with Destiny's toys. "Okay, guy. Let's go."

Destiny stood with his arms crossed, not moving. "I wanna costume. I wanna be in the show."

"You can't. People in the show have to sing. And act."

"I can sing. What do you gots to do to act?"

"Pretend to be someone you aren't," Jake said.

"I can pretend. I pretend I'm a pirate all the time. I—"

"It's too late. All the parts are already taken. You get to be audience."

"Does audience get a costume?"

"No. Come on. It's time to go."

The trip to rehearsals required two vehicles. The

Miata, with Randolph and E.D., left fifteen minutes ahead because they needed to get to the theater in time to set up. Then came Sybil's Volvo station wagon, driven by Cordelia, with Jeremy Bernstein and his accordion, Jake and Destiny and Winston. Usually Destiny sang and talked the whole way to Traybridge. Tonight he sat in the corner of the backseat and sulked. At the time the restful silence seemed like a good thing.

It was only later that Jake realized that a sulky Destiny was *never* a good thing. Wearing the messenger uniform that Randolph said made him look like a UPS delivery man, Jake had just finished whirling Jeannie around and was getting himself ready for the kiss that ended their dance when he smelled something burning. Over Jeannie's shoulder he saw a billowing plume of white smoke.

"Fire!" he yelled.

In the ensuing panic the youngest of the child actors fell off the stage. Her screams combined with Winston's frenzied barking to nearly drown out the contradictory orders being shouted from all directions.

"Call 911!"

"Get out! Get out! Everybody get outside!"

"Find the fire extinguisher!"

"Call 911!"

It was E.D. who found the extinguisher and put out

the fire before any serious damage was done.

It had started in a wastebasket backstage, where Destiny had taken apart the pad of paper, crumpled every sheet into a ball, and set fire to the papers with Jake's lighter. He had found the lighter in the pocket of Jake's pants after Jake had changed into his messenger uniform and gone onstage for his scene.

"I was acting!" Destiny explained when he was found with the incriminating lighter still in his hand. "I was pretending to be Jake, burning down his school. Only I didn't have any gasoline."

Randolph, of course, after decreeing that Destiny was never to have matches, lighters, or even paper in his possession again ever in his entire life, blamed Jake.

Chapter Twenty-one

E.D. had very little time to revel in being a hero. "The show must go on," her father said once it was clear that it could. "Fire's out. No real damage done. Call the next scene."

"The next scene has all the children," E.D. said. "Gretl fell off the stage. Her mother took her to the emergency room."

"We'll do it without her tonight, then. She can catch up next rehearsal."

"There won't be a next rehearsal for her," said the nurse who was playing the role of the housekeeper.

"That was a broken arm."

"We're going to have to find a new Gretl," E.D. told her father.

"That's impossible! No one else who auditioned for that part could possibly play it. That's why I cast her in the first place."

"We'll just have to find someone," E.D. said.

The phone rang early the next morning when E.D. was in the schoolroom, revising the history section of her curriculum. Instead of the Civil War, her fall history project from now on would be World War II, specifically the Nazi occupation of Austria. That way she could count the show as schoolwork. The phone rang again. When nobody had answered it by the third ring, E.D. picked it up. It was Mrs. Montrose, president of the board of the Traybridge Little Theatre. "I want to speak to your father!" the woman said. "I understand there was an arson attempt at the theater last night."

"Not arson," E.D. hastily assured her. "It was purely an accident."

"I have my sources," the woman said, "and they say the fire was deliberately set. Furthermore, a child was injured—"

"It was only a broken arm," E.D. said.

"I wish to speak to Randolph Applewhite immediately."

"I'm sorry, but he's not here," E.D. said. Strictly speaking, this was not a lie. Her father was not in the schoolroom. It was only eight o'clock in the morning. He was upstairs, in bed, sound asleep. "May I take a message?"

"You tell him that I'm canceling the show. From the moment he took over this project, I have had serious doubts about the appropriateness of his choices. But this—this *disaster* is the final straw. The Traybridge Little Theatre is a historic landmark and we came perilously close to losing it. As for injuries, our liability insurance does not—"

E.D. thought fast. "That will be a shock to the television crew that's coming for the opening. I'm sure you know that *The Sound of Music* is expected to be the centerpiece of the story they're putting on network TV."

"I don't care about that; I care about the future of—"

E.D. hurried on. "I was planning to call you this morning, actually. It was the little girl playing Gretl who broke her arm, and if the show *were* able to go on, we would need to replace her. I noticed that your daughter auditioned for that role as well as the role of Brigitta originally. I was hoping you could bring her by to let her audition again. Of course, there would be no point if the show's being canceled. . . ."

There was a long silence, broken only by what sounded like fingernails being tapped on a hard surface.

"Would this be an open audition?"

"Oh no. Only your daughter. My father just wants a chance to hear her again. He told me that none of the others could possibly play the role. In fact, he actually refused to hear any of them again."

"Well . . . well . . ." The tapping went on again for a moment. "When would he need to see her?"

"Perhaps the two of you could come this evening," E.D. said. "After your daughter auditions, you could stay for dinner. We're having fried chicken. The associate producer will be here for dinner as well." These things were both perfectly true. Govindaswami had promised them fried chicken, and Jeremy had taken to introducing himself as associate producer. "You could talk to him about the television project."

This time the pause was considerably shorter. "Dinner. I think we might be able to manage dinner. What time?"

E.D. grinned. "Rehearsal is due to begin at seven. How about coming here at about four-thirty? You and your daughter can meet the producer, your daughter can sing, and then we'll all have dinner."

"All right, then. Four-thirty. But tell your father that there will have to be much stricter control maintained during rehearsals in the future."

"Of course. He was just saying that very thing last night—after the accident." That, too, was true. "You're not to let Destiny out of your sight for an instant!" he had told Jake. When Jake had reminded him that Destiny had done the deed while Jake was onstage, he had threatened to put Destiny on a leash and tie the leash to a theater seat.

When E.D. put down the phone, she sighed. It had worked. But Mrs. Montrose was only the first part of the problem. The second part was Randolph Applewhite.

"Absolutely not!" he said over breakfast when she told him her plan. "I can't possibly use that child as Gretl. Gretl's the youngest. She has to be little and cute. The Montrose kid has a wretched voice, she's not little, and she's definitely not cute. It's completely impossible."

"I thought appearances didn't count," Sybil said, looking up from the hem she was stitching.

"Not when there's talent. That child has no talent."

"At least listen to her," E.D. argued. "They're due to come at four-thirty and they're staying for dinner. If you don't do this, Mrs. Montrose will cancel the show."

"Let her! Better to cancel than to have a Gretl with a voice like a buzz saw."

"No, no, no!" Jeremy Bernstein said. "If the show is canceled, the television piece will be canceled, too. I'll never get another chance to produce for network television. The multiracial *Sound of Music* is the hook the TV execs bought! They won't do the story without the hook."

"Don't let the TV people cancel us!" Cordelia said. "I want to get my bit in about *The Death of Ophelia.*"

"And my gallery showing," Archie said. "And Lucille's new volume of poetry."

Sybil held up the black costume she was hemming. "Do you mean to tell me that you would let the seven million nuns' habits we've made go to waste? Do you mean to tell me that I've given up my writing time and let my masterpiece go totally cold for *nothing?*"

E.D. resumed her attack. "Come on, Dad. Just *listen* to Priscilla Montrose. Talk to her mother over dinner. Maybe you can convince her to let the show go on even if you don't cast her daughter. You have to at least *try*!"

"All right. All right! But I will not, under any circumstances, cast that dreadful girl as Gretl!"

Chapter Twenty-two

hile the others were having breakfast at the main house, Jake, desperate for some time away from Destiny, was in the kitchen at Wisteria Cottage, eating dry Cheerios and drinking a cup of Archie's morning coffee. Every so often he threw a Cheerio at Winston, who snapped it out of the air and swallowed it. Jake had just drifted into a reverie about Jeannie Ng, who had taken Cordelia's place as the most beautiful girl he had ever seen, when he heard the yodeling refrain of "The Lonely Goatherd."

Destiny, he thought. Somewhere nearby. And getting nearer. He was just considering the possibility of barricading himself in his room when Destiny's voice began to fade. He waited. Maybe he was safe after all. After a moment, though, the yodeling began to come closer again. Closer, closer. As Jake pushed his chair back from the table, ready to bolt and run, the voice began to recede again. This went on for some time, fading, coming closer, fading, coming closer. Jake resisted the urge to go see what the kid was doing. Once Destiny caught sight of him, his time alone would be gone for the day.

Suddenly Destiny quit singing. There was a loud yelp, followed shortly by pounding footsteps up the steps and across the front porch. Destiny tore open the screen door and hurtled across the living room and into the kitchen. Moments later hoofbeats sounded on the porch and Wolfie smashed into and then through the screen.

Jake looked up in time to see the goat, that crazed look in his yellow eyes, pieces of screen dangling from his horns, collide with the couch. Winston had begun to bark, and his barking apparently infuriated the goat. When the couch didn't move out of his way, Wolfie butted it again and again and then went totally berserk, knocking over a lamp and an end table, upending the hippopotamus coffee table, crashing into the bookcases, and scattering books and candles in every direction. Jake hurried Destiny into his room, closed the door, and then went after the goat. He managed to grab one horn, but the goat twisted away and charged at him.

Jake leaped out of the way. He snatched the tablecloth off the kitchen table, ignoring the crash of his cereal bowl and coffee mug hitting the floor, and flung the cloth over the goat's head. Blinded, Wolfie knocked over a chair, then bounced off the kitchen table. Jake grabbed the ends of the cloth and held on.

When he had wrestled Wolfie out the door and down off the porch, he managed to get the cloth tied around the goat's neck like a leash. Then, partly dragging and partly shoving, with a still barking Winston following at a safe distance, he got the goat back to the pen and in through the gate. A few moments later Destiny showed up, Hazel walking docilely at his side. Hazel came into the pen after Wolfie. "Stay outside the fence," Jake warned Destiny. Gingerly he untied the cloth and managed to get out of the pen and close the gate just as Wolfie's horns crashed resoundingly into it.

"I was herding the goatses!" Destiny said. "Just like in the song."

"It looked more like Wolfie herding you," Jake told him.

"Wolfie doesn't like to be herded."

"Remember that! Don't try to herd him ever again. Hazel's okay, but you stay away from Wolfie."

At four-thirty Jake and Destiny were in the schoolroom watching a butterfly chrysalis that had begun moving slightly on the thread that held it to its twig when a car pulled up in front of the main house. Through the schoolroom window Jake saw Mrs. Montrose and her daughter get out. As always, Mrs. Montrose's hair was elegantly coiffed. She was dressed in a yellow silk suit. Her daughter, a tall, thin girl of seven or eight, with blond hair braided in two pigtails, was wearing a white sailor dress, shiny white strapped shoes, and socks with white ruffles. They went up the porch stairs and disappeared from view.

A short time later a shrill, piercing voice filled the house with an off-key version of "The Lonely Goatherd."

Destiny, his nose pressed to the aquarium, announced that he could sing it better than that. He was right, Jake realized. He and Destiny had been singing together a whole lot lately, and the practice had made a difference. On the other hand, Destiny had never sounded as bad as Priscilla Montrose.

The chrysalis had cracked open, and something that looked nothing at all like a butterfly was pushing its way out. "Doesn't look like much, does it?" Jake asked. Destiny shook his head. E.D. came in to ask Jake to help set the table for dinner.

"Look, E.D.! That yucky thing was in the criss-liss. What happened to the butterfly?"

"That *is* the butterfly," E.D. said.

"Those black crumply things on its back are its wings," Jake said. "As soon as it pumps them up and they dry out, it'll be able to fly. You'll see."

"I'm not gonna eat dinner then," Destiny said. "I wanna watch it get wings."

Jake felt a little that way himself. He'd actually never seen a butterfly come out of its chrysalis before. On the other hand, he didn't want to miss one of Govindaswami's dinners.

"Don't worry," E.D. said. "We'll be finished eating long before it's ready to fly. It takes ages and ages. You'd get bored waiting."

"Do you promise it's going to be a butterfly?"

"I promise."

Destiny turned to Jake. "Do *you* promisc?"

"I promise."

Chapter Twenty-three

By the time everyone was settled at the table for dinner, the dining room was so jammed with people and extra chairs that it was difficult to move. Winston, who had insisted on settling under the table by Jake's feet, had been banished to the out of doors. E.D., perched on one of the bar stools from the kitchen, had an excellent vantage point for watching the interaction between her father and Mrs. Montrose. But there was none. Her father, at the foot of the table, was avoiding eye contact with anyone. As the serving dishes of rice and lentils, chutney, flatbread, and yogurt sauce were passed, he stayed resolutely focused on serving himself and passing them on.

Mrs. Montrose, squeezed between her daughter and Jeremy Bernstein across the table from E.D., was just as resolutely focused on Jeremy, alternately asking him questions about the life of a TV producer and dropping offhanded remarks about the many roles her daughter had played in Little Theatre productions.

Govindaswami came in from the kitchen with a huge bowl and offered it to Zedediah at the head of the table. "The main dish," he said as he settled in his place nearest the kitchen. "As promised—fried chicken."

When Zedediah dished himself some, E.D. thought it looked pretty much like most of Govindaswami's main dishes—chunks of meat and vegetables in a thick, red sauce. It certainly wasn't like any fried chicken she'd ever seen.

When the bowl reached Mrs. Montrose, she sat for a moment, looking at it. "You did say fried chicken, didn't you?" she asked.

Govindaswami nodded. "Fried chicken. Yes. An old Govindaswami family recipe. My mother made it often, as did her mother and her mother before her."

"Ah! I see. It isn't quite what I expected." Mrs. Montrose spooned some onto her plate next to her rice.

"You'll want some of the yogurt sauce," Govindaswami said.

"No thank you, I'm not particularly fond of yogurt."

"Suit yourself."

Mrs. Montrose spooned a small amount of the chicken onto her daughter's plate and passed the bowl on.

When everyone was served, Zedediah asked them to join hands. "Let us offer heartfelt thanks to Ravi Govindaswami for his fine, rich, and pungent cooking. Thanks as well to the Traybridge Little Theatre for the opportunity to work together to bring a new artistic vision to the stage. And thanks to all the powers that be for the joining here of family, friends, and colleagues, for this abundance of food, of companionship, of"—here he looked directly at Randolph and raised his voice meaningfully—"tact and good sense."

When they dropped hands, E.D. watched her father dig into the food on his plate. She didn't think he'd been listening. Now that she'd watched Priscilla Montrose's audition, she understood his problem. It wasn't just that the girl was too tall to be the littlest von Trapp. It wasn't just her voice. It was everything about her. The girl had stood like a telephone pole—rigid and totally unmoving, with her hands clasped in front of her like some old-fashioned opera star, and all through the yodeling part had sung every syllable as if it were a separate word. *Oh. Ho. Lay. Dee. Odl. Lee.*

Oh. It didn't sound anything at all like yodeling. The lines she read were even worse. She could see why he thought it would be better to let the show be canceled than to have her in it!

E.D. looked over at Mrs. Montrose. She was just taking her first bite of chicken. She chewed once and her eyes grew very wide. She looked wildly from side to side like a trapped animal, her face going a deep, rich pink. Her eyes watered. She gave a little squeak, put her napkin up to her lips, swallowed, and snatched at her water glass, gulping down its contents without pausing for breath. Beads of sweat had broken out on her forehead. "Very—very—*interesting*," she said in a strangulated voice. She smiled at Govindaswami. Then she reached for her daughter's water and drank that, too.

"The yogurt sauce is quite cooling," Lucille said.

"If you are finding it a little too spicy for your palate," Govindaswami observed, "you will discover that water does not help. It only dilutes the acid."

"No, no!" Mrs. Montrose said after a moment. "Not too spicy. It's—delicious." She wiped her forehead with her napkin. "I'm just—ah—very thirsty."

Priscilla Montrose had been picking at her rice. Now she raised a forkful of chicken. Her mother reached to stop her, but the girl had already popped the chicken into her mouth. She chewed, and began to shriek. "Hot! Hot! Mommee-ee-ee, hot!" She spit the chicken back onto her plate and grabbed for her water glass. It was empty. She went on shrieking.

"Manners, Prissy dear, manners!" Mrs. Montrose said, patting her daughter's back, her face getting pinker by the moment.

Sybil, sitting on the little girl's other side, reached for the pitcher of grape Kool-Aid in front of Destiny. "Try this," she said, pouring it into the empty water glass. "Sugar cuts the burning."

Priscilla stopped shrieking long enough to gulp down the Kool-Aid. Sybil filled her glass again. Mrs. Montrose held out her own glass. "That looks so good. Perhaps you might pour me a little as well."

Wimps, E.D. thought. The chicken wasn't nearly as hot as some of Govindaswami's dishes. She passed a plate of bread across the table. "She might like the bread. And the rice is good with a little fruit chutney."

"I'm terribly sorry," Mrs. Montrose said. "She's just not used to—*ethnic* cooking."

After that the meal went fairly smoothly, E.D. thought. Priscilla ate nothing but bread, washed down with grape Kool-Aid. Mrs. Montrose, still a little pink in the face, withdrew from the conversation. Smiling and nodding, she kept moving the chicken around on her plate, but E.D. noticed that she was careful to actually eat only rice that hadn't been contaminated by any of the sauce.

The other adults kept up a constant stream of

positive chatter about *The Sound of Music*. They talked about how well things were going with the sets and costumes, how successful the run was bound to be. Jeremy mentioned several times how interested the TV executives were about the way it had been cast, and how impressed they were that such a groundbreaking production was being done by a theater in Traybridge, North Carolina. Randolph remained absolutely quiet.

Twice Destiny got up from the table and went off to the schoolroom to check on the butterfly. When Jake explained what he was doing, Priscilla Montrose asked if she could go with him next time. Her mother took a bite of bread and nodded vaguely.

Destiny finished his chicken, topped with liberal portions of yogurt sauce, drank the rest of his Kool-Aid, and got up again. "Come on!" he said to Priscilla. "Betcha he can fly now."

It wasn't until Govindaswami announced ginger saffron ice cream for dessert that everyone noticed that Destiny and Priscilla had not returned. Jake was sent to find them. In moments he was back. "They're not in the schoolroom."

"Where do you suppose they went?" Mrs. Montrose asked, her voice carefully polite, but tinged with alarm.

Before anyone could respond, the answer was clear. From outside came the sound of two voices, one of them shrill and off-key, singing "The Lonely Goatherd."

"Uh-oh," Jake said.

Randolph sat up a little straighter, listening.

Jake got up from the table and started toward the front of the house. "I'd just better make sure Destiny hasn't—"

He was interrupted by a blood-curdling shriek. The singing had stopped. Wild barking had started.

"Mommy! Mommy! Help! Mommy!"

Mrs. Montrose rose from her chair and started to push her way around the table toward the sound of her daughter's voice. Zedediah, Archie, and Sybil all leaped up and started for the doorway. As they reached it, Priscilla Montrose, sobbing now, came running in, squeezed her way between them, and dove past E.D. and under the table, headed for her mother. Immediately behind her came Wolfie, and behind Wolfie came Winston, barking steadily. Wolfie butted Archie out of the way, then Sybil, then smashed into the table. The jolt tipped over all the glasses and the pitcher of Kool-Aid.

A black swallowtail butterfly fluttered into the dining room, drifting serenely above the chaos.

Chapter Twenty-four

Jake and Archie each managed to get hold of one of Wolfie's horns and together dragged the struggling goat out of the house. "We were only herding Hazel, just like you said," Destiny told Jake, as he hurried alongside them toward the goat pen. "But Wolfie got out too."

"I'm getting a padlock for that gate!" Archie said.

By the time they got back to the house, everyone except Randolph stood on the porch as Mrs. Montrose and Priscilla headed for their car. The yellow silk suit, Priscilla's white sailor dress, and her ruffled socks were stained with purple.

"We're terribly sorry," Sybil was saying. "You'll be sure to send us the cleaning bill, won't you?"

"No, no, now it wasn't your fault," Mrs. Montrose said. Jake thought she was maintaining her calm with a supreme effort of will. There was an edge to her voice that bordered on the hysterical. "Besides, nothing will take these stains out. We'll just . . . we'll just . . ." Her voice dwindled and stopped.

"My father will call you," E.D. said.

Govindaswami's usually cheerful face was creased with a frown. "You didn't get your ice cream."

"Another time, perhaps," Mrs. Montrose managed to say as she got into her car and closed the door firmly.

The rehearsal that night didn't include any of Jake's scenes, so when the others left for the theater or scattered to work on costumes or sets, he and Destiny helped Govindaswami clean up the mess in the dining room. Afterward, Jake caught the butterfly, which Destiny had named Blackie, and tried to persuade Destiny to turn it loose outdoors.

"What if it rains?" Destiny asked.

"It won't. And even if it did, butterflies stay out in the rain all the time."

Destiny, his lower lip stuck out and his arms folded firmly across his chest, shook his head. "I want him to stay in my room tonight. Winston stays in your room; I want Blackie to stay in mine."

"But he needs to eat! We have to put him outside where he can find flowers."

"It's dark outside. He won't be able to see them."

Jake remembered the website that had given the recipe for feeding butterflies. What had been in it? Soy sauce, he remembered. They had that. And milk. What else? Then he remembered. "Can't feed him," he told Destiny. "We don't have any Gatorade."

"We gots Kool-Aid!" Destiny said.

"It isn't the same. Besides, Wolfie spilled it all."

"There's more. We can make more."

Sugar syrup, Jake remembered then. You could also feed butterflies sugar syrup. "We don't need Kool-Aid."

"What do we need?"

"Sugar and water."

"We gots that!" Destiny said.

So, when Govindaswami had gone off to do his evening meditations, Jake let Blackie loose in the kitchen. Immediately, the butterfly fluttered to the floor. Winston's whole body went rigid, his ears up, his tail straight out behind, his eyes riveted on the butterfly's slowly moving wings. For a long moment he remained that way, so still he might have been carved of stone. Then he launched himself at the butterfly and pounced, his heavy body lurching into the air and coming down where the butterfly had been. Destiny screamed. Luckily the butterfly had fluttered up toward the counter.

There followed a skirmish—the butterfly landing on the floor, Winston charging after it and pouncing just as it flew up. Destiny yelled at Winston to stop, and Jake did his best to catch the dog's collar. But the awkward, ungainly dog, his hunting instincts fully engaged, had suddenly become a canine athlete. He leaped into the air, trying to catch the butterfly on the wing. Jake had just grabbed the net, hoping to catch the butterfly and get it safely away from Winston's snapping jaws, when it fluttered up toward the ceiling and then landed on the philodendron plant that hung by the window. There it stayed, opening and closing its wings gently as if the whole thing had been a game that it had easily won.

Jake put Winston outside, then put some water on to boil.

"Why are you making it hot? It'll burn Blackie's tongue!"

"We won't let Blackie have it till it cools. Hot water will dissolve the sugar faster," Jake said. When the water boiled, Jake put a cup of sugar into a bowl and poured in some water. He stirred awhile, then poured in some more. "I think that should do it," he said.

Destiny frowned. "Blackie won't like that. Butterflies like flowers. That isn't pretty like flowers." Destiny climbed onto a stool and got a packet of grape Kool-Aid out of the cupboard. "We can make it purple. That's pretty."

Jake shrugged. If butterflies could eat soy sauce and Gatorade, grape Kool-Aid probably wouldn't hurt them.

Destiny dumped the package of drink powder into the bowl and Jake stirred it. "That's good!" Destiny said, looking at the deep purple syrup. "Pretty."

Jake nodded. "Blackie will love it."

Jake poured a little into a saucer and set it on the counter. "Now that'll be cool in a minute and he'll come and sit on the edge and drink some. I *think*."

They waited. And waited. Blackie didn't move off the philodendron. Finally, Jake put his hand out in front of the butterfly, thinking he might shoo it off the plant and down to the counter. To his surprise, it stepped onto his fingers. Gently and carefully, he moved his hand down next to the saucer and the butterfly began uncoiling its long, black tongue. In a moment, the butterfly stepped delicately off Jake's hand and onto the edge of the saucer, then stretched its tongue like a long straw into the purple liquid.

"It's working! It's working!" Destiny said. "He's drinking!"

Jake could hardly believe his eyes. He wished he had E.D.'s camera.

After a while Blackie coiled his tongue back up and

fluttered away from the saucer. He flew around the kitchen a couple of times and then landed on Destiny's shoulder. Destiny's eyes got very big and round. "Look, Jake. He likes me!"

"Of *course* he does. Now, if you are very quiet and walk very carefully, maybe he'll ride up to your room with you." He picked up the butterfly net, just in case, and followed as Destiny took tiny baby steps out of the kitchen and up the stairs.

Three hours later Jake was in the schoolroom going over his lines when Randolph, E.D., Jeremy, and Cordelia got home. E.D. came in to see if any of the other butterflies had come out. She didn't believe him about Blackie and the Kool-Aid. "You'll see for yourself tomorrow," he told her.

"Where's the butterfly now?" she asked.

"Somewhere in Destiny's room."

"Is Destiny asleep?"

"He wasn't when I came down a little while ago. He was singing to Blackie. He says Blackie is the bestest pet he's ever had except that he can't pet him. I tried to get him to go to sleep about an hour ago, but it was no good. He's used to being up till rehearsal's over."

"It's a good thing."

"Why?"

E.D. sighed. "Dad's decided on the replacement Gretl."

"Not Priscilla Montrose?"

"This is Randolph Applewhite we're talking about here. Of *course* he's not going to use Priscilla Montrose. He's going to call Mrs. Montrose first thing tomorrow morning and tell her his choice. When she hears it, she'll cancel the show. He'd rather have a musical with good singers canceled than one with lousy singers that actually happens."

"Who's he going to cast?"

"Destiny."

Jake felt his jaw drop. "He can't cast Destiny. Gretl's a girl!"

"He's the director; he can do anything he likes. He's going to turn Gretl into a boy and call him Hans. Destiny's little enough to be cute, which is more than you could say about Priscilla Montrose. There's nothing in the script that can't work that way." E.D. sighed deeply. "It won't matter, though. The whole reason Mrs. Montrose hasn't canceled it already, the whole reason she didn't get up and leave the minute she took a bite of Govindaswami's chicken, was that she thought her daughter was going to get to be on network television. The minute she finds out that isn't going to happen, it'll all be over."

Jake felt his stomach clench. *No!* It could not all be over. Enough bad things had happened to him this year! He was going to do this. He was going to play Rolf. He and Jeannie Ng were going to sing their duet and dance and he was going to kiss her. He was going to hold a gun on the von Trapps when they were escaping. And to do all this he was going to cut off his scarlet hair and take off his eyebrow ring and all his earrings.

"It's *your* fault," E.D. told him. "You're the one who taught Destiny to sing. If he hadn't heard Destiny, he would have *had* to cast Priscilla."

"I didn't teach Destiny; I just sang with him. All it was was practice. Maybe all of you can sing."

"The thing is, it doesn't matter. It's all over."

Jake thought about what had happened ever since Randolph Applewhite had asked his family for help. And then he smiled. Little by little, he felt his stomach unclenching. E.D. was wrong. How could she, an actual member of the Applewhite family, possibly think it could all be over? All of them, even the invisible Hal, had put their whole *selves* into this show by now. Not just family, either. Bernstein. Govindaswami. It didn't matter anymore that it was Randolph's show, that it was a project nobody else had wanted anything to do with. Everybody was involved in it now.

And the way these people got involved was like nothing he'd ever seen before. They might moan and groan and grouch and complain about how much there was to do, but they put everything else aside and *did it*. "Passion," Govindaswami had said. That was it. What the Applewhites did they did with passion. They cared about the show now the way some people cared about flying around the world in a balloon or sailing across the ocean alone or climbing Mt. Everest. "She may cancel it, but it'll happen anyway. Some way or another, it'll happen. You'll see. I'll make you a bet."

E.D. was an Applewhite after all, he thought. She knew better than to take the bet.

Chapter Twenty-five

E.D. woke early, dreading her father's call to Mrs. Montrose. She tried for a while to go back to sleep, but she couldn't. Finally, she decided that she didn't want to face catastrophe on an empty stomach, so she pulled on jeans and a T-shirt and headed downstairs to fix herself something to eat.

Destiny was already up. She could hear him in the kitchen singing "Do-Re-Mi." Dad's right, she thought. Destiny *can* sing a whole lot better than Priscilla Montrose. She hoped what Jake had said would turn out to be true, that there would be a show for Destiny to sing in. When she got to the kitchen, it was the butterfly she noticed first, standing on a saucer full of purple syrup, its wings moving delicately, its long tube of a tongue arched into the liquid.

Then she noticed a puddle of purple syrup on the counter and a bowl in the middle of the puddle. And then she noticed Destiny. He had a purple-stained towel around his shoulders and purple syrup in his hair and running down over his ears and neck.

He stopped singing and grinned at her. "Isn't he *beautiful*? His name is Blackie, and he stayed in my room the whole night. He roded down on my shoulder and I fed him. He's the bestest pet I ever had. He—"

"Why did you put syrup in your hair?"

"That lady said Kool-Aid won't wash out. Jake washes all my other colors out. Now my hair gets to stay purple like Jake's gets to stay red."

E.D. had her brother on a stool by the sink with his head under the faucet when her father came in. As much of a mess as the sticky purple syrup had made, it had not turned Destiny's hair purple. Almost all the color had washed out, leaving his white blond hair with just the tiniest tinge of lavender. His hands and his ears were another thing altogether. They were stained a deep, purply gray, and his fingernails were almost black.

Randolph stood in the doorway and looked. E.D. braced herself for his reaction. But her father let out a long, dramatic sigh. "I suppose this is what comes of getting up in the middle of the night," he muttered as he set about making a pot of coffee. The butterfly fluttered up to the philodendron.

"Might as well get it over with," Randolph said when he'd drunk his coffee. He went off to make the phone call to Mrs. Montrose. E.D. scrubbed and scrubbed Destiny's hands and fingernails with soap and a nailbrush until most of the color was gone. But she dared not take a brush to his ears. They were apparently going to have to fade on their own.

When her father came back ten minutes later, he was shaking his head. "It would have been interesting, integrating a purple-eared boy named Hans into the show."

"She canceled it?" E.D. asked.

"She canceled it."

"Did you try to reason with her?"

"Reason with her? She started babbling like a maniac, and I couldn't get a word in edgewise. She said I had violated her trust and the trust of an innocent and impressionable eight-year-old child. What do you suppose she meant by that? I never promised that wretched little girl would get the part."

E.D. had never fully explained what she'd told the woman on the phone when she invited her to dinner. She decided this was not a good time to do so.

"I tell you, the more that woman talked, the more

berserk she got. Something about fried chicken and false pretenses and crazed wild animals endangering her daughter's life. I couldn't get her to stop, so finally I just hung up on her."

As the news of the cancellation spread around Wit's End, it was as if someone had lit a string of firecrackers. One after another came the explosions. Nobody blamed Mrs. Montrose. They blamed Randolph. "You never once think of anyone except yourself!" she heard her mother say. "It's not as if it's a Broadway production. What harm could the little girl have done the show?" All E.D. caught of her father's answer was the phrase "artistic integrity."

Zedediah, who was usually the solid rock under the family's waves, raged about the customers he had put on hold in order to build sets instead of furniture and the cost of the raw materials they had used from the wood shop. He sounded more like Paulie than himself. Archie yelled about not having had time to finish two of the pieces for his gallery show. Cordelia was the most dramatic. She held her hands out to her father. "Look at them. Just look! My fingers have *bled* and I'm practically going blind from making ruffles for little girls' dresses. Besides all those ruffles—*and* the choreography, *and* teaching twenty-five people with two left feet how to waltz—I have hemmed four nuns' habits. Do you know how far it is around the bottom of a nun's habit?"

Jeremy Bernstein shrieked when he was told. Thanks to Randolph Applewhite, he said, his television career was over. "First my car, now my career—totaled. Totaled!" Randolph pointed out that his TV career hadn't actually started yet—and Jeremy burst into tears. Jake just clenched his fists. His face went almost as red as his hair, and he stormed off across the field with Winston following. Lucille, being Lucille, did not explode or shriek or cry. She got a faraway look in her eyes and went off to meditate.

Govindaswami was the only one entirely unmoved by the news. "Aaahhh," he said gravely. "This will be a good thing. Everything works for the highest good. Always this is so. You will see. The Universe works in mysterious ways."

E.D. went to the schoolroom and watched two more butterflies struggle to break free of their gray-brown cases. She couldn't help thinking about what Govindaswami had said. It seemed stupid. Worse, it was *mean*. Everybody was miserable, and he was telling them that their misery was perfectly okay. How could any good, let alone the highest good, come from wasting all that time and effort? And what could be good about having to call people who had their hearts set on being in the show and telling them it was all off?

Her father was going to call the leads, but as stage manager she was the one who had to call the minor actors. She could hardly bring herself to think about it, much less do it. Govindaswami talked like somebody out of one of those old black-and-white movies, she thought, where everything always turned around just in time for a happy ending.

It was when she thought about those movies that the idea popped into her mind. Her father had rented one of them once about a theater company that lost its theater. They'd put on the show in a barn instead. Wit's End had a barn. A big barn. They parked cars in it sometimes, and the riding mower was there. But when it was empty, it was really quite a lot like a theater, except that it didn't have a stage. Or seats. Or lights. Maybe they could fix that. They'd have to build a stage and find some lights and some sound equipment and some chairs for the audience. They'd have to do publicity. Sell tickets.

Could they?

If they could, Jeremy wouldn't have to give up his television career. The network people might like the story even better this way—art struggling against impossible odds. Today was Friday, October tenth. The original opening had been set for the twenty-fourth. Two weeks away. Fourteen days. E.D. went to find her father.

Chapter Twenty-six

Jake had found a crumpled cigarette in the bottom of his duffel bag and gone out into the woods to smoke it, Winston tagging loyally along. It hadn't helped. He realized with considerable shock that he didn't really like the taste smoking left in his mouth, that he'd *never* liked it. After two drags he crushed out the cigarette. He swore. He kicked the trunk of a tree. He imagined a house—Mrs. Montrose's house—going up in flames. The Traybridge Little Theatre blowing up and then settling in a cloud of dust like those buildings they showed being demolished on television. Winston had flopped down a considerable distance away and was eyeing him warily.

"Okay, okay," he said to the dog. "I probably wouldn't do those things even if I could." The dog came no closer. "Let's walk."

When the two of them got back, having wandered the whole of Wit's End, the barn doors were open and the cars had been moved out into the driveway. Zedediah, riding the lawn mower, was coming out, while Archie and someone Jake had never seen before were going in, carrying a stack of two-by-fours. Cordelia and Lucille, both with handkerchiefs tied over their hair, were coming from the main house carrying brooms, mops, and buckets. Jake felt a kind of electricity in the air that was how it must be when an army was getting ready for an all-out assault.

"Go to the schoolroom and get your assignment," Cordelia called to him. "I think you're supposed to help Archie and Hal."

Archie and Hal? That stranger whose back he had seen going into the barn must have been Hal—out of his room and into the daylight. He stood for a moment, watching the barn doors, and soon the two came out again. Hal was just about Jake's size, dressed, as Jake was, in black—black boots, black pants, and a black turtleneck. His long, reddish brown hair was pulled back into a ponytail, and he sported a goatee that was a scragglier replica of Randolph's. Hal Applewhite, fifteen-year-old sculptor, looked like a cross between his father and his older sister, except that he had a really bad case of acne. Whatever was going on, Jake thought, it must be big to bring Hal out. Very, very big.

Over the next ten days it turned out to be bigger than Jake could have imagined. The show *would* go on, if it took everyone's dying breath to make it happen. Every member of the cast agreed to stay with the show. For most of them what changed was little more than geography. Instead of going to Traybridge for rehearsals, they now came to Wit's End. What changed for the Applewhites was something else again.

Jake had thought that he knew something about the Applewhites and passion. But nothing had prepared him for what happened when all of them, all at the same time, became totally obsessed with the same thing. What had seemed like hard work before now looked like a sort of happy, restful vacation. Gone was any consideration of larks and owls. Work went on day and night. Sleep was relegated to a nap here or there. Jake gave up on his hair altogether; he needed every moment of sleep he could get. He barely had time for showers, let alone for gelling his hair into points.

The whole of Wit's End was transformed. The barn became command central, where the basic work of creating a theater from scratch went on. Trucks delivered rented folding chairs; rented, borrowed, or scavenged lighting and sound equipment; and lumber. Lots and lots of lumber. At one end of the barn a stage was built, and the loft became the light and sound booth. Wisteria Cottage became the costume shop, with Jake's room serving as dressing room and costume storage. Jake was given a cot in Zedediah's cottage, where he and Winston shared the living room with Paulie. The wood shop, of course, was the scene shop. Rehearsals were held in the dance studio. Destiny was moved in with Hal to free up his room, and Govindaswami and Bernstein doubled up in Dogwood Cottage so that Sweet Gum Cottage could be turned into a kind of dormitory to house the people who showed up to lend a hand. It seemed that Randolph knew an almost infinite number of theater people who were between jobs at any given moment. They came in waves, staying for as many days as they could spare and seeming every bit as obsessed while they were there as the Applewhites.

Govindaswami continued to cook, but no longer did work stop for meals. He took the food to the barn, to the wood shop, to Wisteria Cottage, to wherever people were at work, with the help of Destiny and his red wagon. The delivery man from the lumberyard, who happened to arrive one day when shrimp vindaloo was being set out on a plank between two sawhorses, fell instantly in love with Indian cuisine. He ate two plates full and then came back when his delivery shift was over to help, bringing two friends with him. In return for all they could eat of whatever dinner was being served, the three of them came back for four days in a row to build risers to accommodate folding chairs for an audience of one hundred and fifty.

There was something for everyone to do, including Destiny, who became a kind of message and delivery service, scurrying all over Wit's End with his wagon, talking or singing nonstop as he went. Sybil and Jeremy took over marketing and publicity, writing press releases and churning out advertising circulars that labeled the production "The most exciting piece of musical theater ever to appear on a North Carolina stage."

Jake did a little of everything. One moment he would be helping to build the stage, the next he would be hanging lights or running cables. For two days he and Zedediah scoured the countryside for props, and he found himself learning what could have been found in an Austrian household in the 1930s and what could not. It took half a day of going from antiques shop to flea market to used furniture store to find the right sort of telephone for the von Trapp living room. The owner of the shop where they finally found it had read about the production in the newspaper and agreed to let them borrow it in return for a pair of tickets to opening night.

Mrs. Montrose had called the Traybridge paper to

announce the cancellation of the show a moment after she'd spoken to Randolph. The reporter had called Randolph to get his side, and the story had been growing ever since. It was picked up by newspapers across the state, and then television news reporters began showing up with camera crews and getting underfoot. Two versions began to emerge, each with its own hero and its own villain. One had Randolph Applewhite as a crusading New York radical attempting to destroy the grand old traditions of the South while Mrs. Montrose staunchly defended them. The other called Randolph a symbol of the broadening culture of the New South and Mrs. Montrose a throwback to the bad old days.

"They're turning it from an artistic story into a political one!" Randolph complained.

"Publicity is publicity," Bernstein said. "The important thing is to fill the seats!"

One gray and drizzly afternoon Jake was coming out of the barn with a light that had a broken clamp when a reporter stopped him. "You're the kid who burned down a school in Rhode Island, aren't you? Did you have anything to do with the fire at the Traybridge Little Theatre?"

"No comment," Jake said, and ducked back into the barn.

Chapter Twenty-seven

E.D. looked up from the computer screen as one of the five butterflies currently residing in the schoolroom fluttered past her to land next to another on a slice of overripe cantelope. It sank its long tongue into the soft orange flesh. Two others were drinking from a saucer of sugar syrup on Jake's desk. Since the incident with Destiny's hair, coloring of any kind had been banned from the butterflies' food supply. Destiny's ears had faded to a pale lavender.

The Butterfly Project, and the time when it had

been so important to her, seemed very far away. It had been twelve days since the show and the barn (now called Wit's End Playhouse) had completely taken over their lives. She couldn't even remember what her curriculum notebook would have had her doing this week.

She yawned. Tonight was the first dress rehearsal, and she'd been up since five-thirty. It was raining, which would cause trouble if it kept up all day. The way they'd had to build the stage, actors who had to exit on one side and come back onstage from the other had to run around the outside of the barn. No one had thought that would be a problem, because it hadn't rained more than about fifty drops in two and a half months. This part of North Carolina was in the midst of the worst drought in living memory.

But Zedediah had said that one thing he'd learned for certain in seventy years of living was not to trust the weather. On one of his prop runs he had bought two dozen umbrellas and stationed a dozen at each exit so an actor could grab one on the way out, run around, and drop it off on the way in. The stage crew, the prop crew, and the dressers, most of whom had been recruited from Traybridge High School, also had to run around the barn from one side of the stage to the other, but they were not going to be allowed to use the umbrellas. They had no costumes to protect. E.D. was writing a notice to explain the rain plan now.

She ran over her to-do list for the day one more time and smiled. It was actually beginning to look as if this impossible idea would work. If it did, she would have had a whole lot to do with it, not just because it was her idea in the first place, but because from the moment her father agreed to doing the show in the barn, she had focused everything she had on getting things organized and keeping them that way. She had found out from the adults what needed to be done to get both the barn and the show ready for opening night and then made a series of charts and sign-up sheets and schedules. These had taken over the schoolroom where the maps and papers and the butterfly chart used to be. Now one wall was devoted to barn renovation. Another was for the actors, with rehearsal schedules, costume fittings, and lists of each actor's personal props. A third was for tech crews. She had a master list in a notebook she kept with her, and she kept all the charts and schedules updated so anyone could check them anytime.

The fourth wall she had reserved for clippings and Internet printouts from local newspapers. The story kept changing shape. At first it had been about her father and Mrs. Montrose. Then Jake got to be in the middle of it. One local weekly told how working on the show was turning a delinquent around. But the Traybridge paper, under the headline "Can Traybridge Support Two Theaters?," suggested that the theater being built at Wit's End "by northern newcomers" was intended to put the Traybridge Little Theatre out of business. It speculated on the possible connection between the burning of a school in Rhode Island and a "fire of uncertain origin" at the Little Theatre.

Jake said bad press didn't bother him, but Randolph had fumed about the unfairness of the second story and the TV news reporters who picked it up. "We never even *thought* of making a theater till they canceled us!" Lucille, who was both heading the costume crew and taking ticket orders on the phone, said that right after the story appeared there was a huge increase in the number of ticket orders. Publicity, as Jeremy had said, was publicity. Sybil added that not only were news stories good advertising, they were free. The ads running in the very same papers were costing a lot of "Petunia Grantham" money.

Whether it was the free publicity or the ads, tickets were selling better than anyone had expected. With only three days to go till the opening, they had two sold-out houses and decent-sized audiences for the other performances. Almost half the opening night seats would go to the media and to people who had donated props or costumes or helped with the show, and at least a third of the others were going to families of the actors. It didn't bring in much money to have that many complimentary tickets, but it guaranteed a full house for the most important night of the run, the night the network people would be there.

This was the day the television crew was arriving, and Jeremy had been such a wreck when he came into the kitchen for breakfast that Govindaswami had told him he wasn't going to be allowed to eat till he'd spent at least half an hour meditating. Then Sybil had insisted that everyone take a little time from their other jobs to clean the house. "I won't have the world think that the author of the Petunia Grantham mysteries lives in a pigsty." Now the house was at least moderately presentable. The Applewhites wouldn't look like slobs as long as the cameras stayed away from the closets.

The barn was almost ready. They'd been rehearsing on the newly built stage for three days now. Zedediah was overseeing the last of the construction work. And Hal, with help from Cordelia, was painting the sets.

A butterfly landed on E.D.'s hand, and she waved it gently away. They had no fear of humans at all, these butterflies. Outside she heard a car pull to a stop. After a moment, Winston began barking. That must be the television people, she thought. Hurriedly she printed out the notice about the umbrellas and went to pin it up on the wall. As she did, she heard someone come into the schoolroom behind her. She turned her head to see who it was and was so startled that she stabbed the pushpin into her finger. She yelped.

"That bad, huh?"

Jake was standing there in his usual black T-shirt and black pants. But that was all that was usual about him. Gone was the eyebrow ring, gone were all the earrings. And gone was the scarlet hair. He had a dark brown crew cut now, so short his scalp showed through. Behind him Winston stood, making low growling sounds.

"So what do you think?" Jake said. "Could I make it in the SS?"

Chapter Twenty-eight

Winston was so unsettled by the change in Jake's appearance that he wouldn't come close enough to be petted. A patch of hair at the back of his neck and another at the base of his tail stood up, and he stayed about two feet away, following Jake as always but growling suspiciously the whole time. An hour later, when the television people arrived in a van bristling with antennae and satellite dishes, the dog was still so edgy that he didn't just bark at the van. When the crew got out, he actually rushed at them, snapping at sneakers and pants legs. Jake had to go find some liver treats and lure him into the schoolroom.

The liver treats helped. In no time Winston was stretched at his feet in his usual way, his nose on his outstretched paws, snoring softly. Jake watched from the window as cameras and lights and cables and sound equipment were unpacked and carted into the house. He was just as glad to be safely away from the action. He'd told everyone he didn't mind bad press, but it wasn't absolutely true. He wanted to be known as an actor now, not the bad kid from the city, and you never knew what the media would say about you.

Jeremy Bernstein had come running the moment he heard the van in the driveway. Jake watched him introduce himself, shaking hands with everyone who got out of the van. It was obvious he didn't know any of these people, and they had no idea who he was or what he was doing there. It wasn't really clear what the title of associate producer meant. It looked to Jake as if Bernstein was mostly in the way, darting around among the crew like an enthusiastic puppy. Destiny arrived, too, and had the good sense to stay back and just watch, though Jake could tell by the way his mouth was working steadily that he was talking the whole time. Asking questions, probably. Nobody seemed to be answering them.

Eventually a limousine arrived and a man with a clipboard got out and called to Bernstein. That had to be Jeremy's friend. The two of them conferred for a while, and then the man with the clipboard opened the limousine door and held it while a short-haired blond woman in a red suit got out. Marcia Manning. Jake had seen her on TV so often it seemed as if he knew her. Except that on TV she always seemed perky and sweet and friendly. Even without being able to hear what anyone was saying, he could see that there was nothing perky or sweet or friendly about her now.

She pointed here, gestured there, and people who were doing one thing when she got out suddenly started doing something else. The man with the clipboard began flipping through his papers, looking more and more harried. She spoke to Bernstein and he rushed into the house and returned a few moments later with a bottle of water, which she snatched from his hand and began drinking as she made her way up the steps and onto the porch.

Jake was in the barn, helping to set up folding chairs, when E.D. came to find Winston. "The wicked witch of the west wants them to get pictures of all the animals," she explained. "Mom says you'd better come, too. The camera guys are all spooked about Winston since he tried to bite them. Is he okay? Has he gotten over your haircut yet?"

"Liver treats," Jake said, and followed E.D. back to

the house, Winston in his usual place a few steps behind.

"All the adults have been interviewed already and gone back to work," she told him as they went. "Mom's interview was the longest, and Dad's all grumpy. They aren't going to interview us kids, except Cordelia. I think the wicked witch has us classified with the animals. Sort of like decorations for background shots."

There were enough cables snaked across the floor in the living room to make walking treacherous. Some very large, very bright lights were focused on the couch and the overstuffed chair, where Marcia Manning was sitting looking over some note cards. A blue-jean-clad man was dabbing at her face with a large makeup brush. Paulie's t-perch had been brought in and set up behind the couch. Paulie was busy eating peanuts and dropping their shells on the floor. Jeremy and the man with the clipboard hovered in the background, whispering to each other.

"Where's that girl with the dog?" Marcia Manning asked, batting away the man with the makeup brush. She caught sight of E.D. "Oh, *there* you are!"

When she saw Winston, she squealed. "He's perfect! Just perfect! Everybody loves basset hounds. Here, dog. Get over here in the light, dog." Winston started toward her. When she reached toward him, he sat, well out of range of her red painted fingernails. She waved toward the corner of the room. "Come over here, little boy—" Jake saw Destiny now, sitting cross-legged on the floor. "What's-your-name—you with the lavender ears." Destiny got up and came toward her with an expression on his face Jake had never seen before. He looked cowed. Almost frightened. "Pat the doggie for us," the woman said, her voice suddenly high and sing-songy. "Nice doggie. Get him to wag his tail."

She pointed to a cameraman. "Get a good angle on that. See if you can get the parrot in the shot, too. All the trouble they'll have bleeping the bloody parrot out of the interviews, we should get him in whenever we can—he's great background color."

Then she noticed Jake. "Who's this?" She waggled a hand at the man with the clipboard. "Chuck? Who's this? Anybody know who this is?"

"Jake," Destiny said. It was the first word he'd said. What had these people done to him?

"The delinquent? No, no. Can't be." She checked her notes and turned to Chuck again. "You said the Semple kid has scarlet hair and body piercings."

Chuck flipped through the papers on his clipboard. "That's true. We got some footage from some local news program when he burned the school."

"Didn't look anything like this, did he?"

"You could ask me," Jake said to her. "I do talk. The answer is yes. It's me. Jake Semple. The actor."

"Well, *that'll* wreck the visuals," she said. A man

with a camera on his shoulder had started toward Jake, and she waved him off. "No point getting him looking like that—and scrap the interview, Chuck. We'll just run the old footage if we need something."

Chuck threw down the clipboard. "I don't suppose you care what *I* want, Marcia." A cameraman picked up the clipboard and handed it back to him.

"Of course I do, Chuckie dear. I respect every pearl that falls from your mouth. But right now you should go out and get some tape of the goats. Before it starts raining again. I'm going to get some coffee."

She got up and headed toward the kitchen, where Jake could hear Govindaswami clattering dishes and humming cheerily to himself. Chuck swore and Paulie repeated his words and added a few of his own. "Smart bird," the man said, as Jeremy led him and one of the cameramen outside.

"That lady told me to shut up!" Destiny said.

"It's a good thing for her it wasn't during Mom's interview," E.D. said.

"How's it been going?" Jake asked.

E.D. shrugged. "She asked lots of questions about what everybody does—the furniture and the poetry and the books. And the Creative Academy. Dad talked about *The Sound of Music*, of course. And the barn. But I don't think it's going the way Jeremy and the producer guy planned. It's sort of like she's just getting a whole lot of talk and a whole lot of pictures and somebody'll have to figure out what to do with it all later. Dad says he's going to demand to see the edited tape before they air it, but Jeremy doesn't think that'll happen."

Marcia Manning came back from the kitchen, holding a big mug, which she waved at the few crew members who were still in the room, fussing with equipment. "The kitchen guru says you can all come get coffee." The makeup man started toward her with his brush. "Later, Henry! Can't you see there aren't any cameras?" She sank onto the couch, leaned back into the cushions, and kicked off her shoes, cradling the coffee mug in both hands. She looked at Jake, E.D., and Destiny. "Scram, kids. I need a little private time. And take the mutt with you." She closed her eyes and let out a deep sigh.

E.D. opened her mouth to say something, but Jake shook his head at her. He pointed. One of the butterflies had fluttered in from the schoolroom and was heading toward the couch. It swooped up and then down again, circled the woman's head twice, and then landed delicately on one of the hands that held the mug.

There was a bloodcurdling shriek from Marcia Manning, quickly picked up and repeated by Paulie. The coffee mug leaped upward, sending coffee toward the ceiling and then back down onto woman and couch. There were more shrieks and curses as

Winston launched himself onto the couch, landed on Marcia Manning, and put his front feet on her shoulders as he snapped at the butterfly that was circling her head. The butterfly flew off toward the kitchen.

"Get this monster off me!" she yelled.

But Winston had already jumped down and was following the butterfly, making little leaps as he went.

"Chuck! Henry! Get in here! Where the—" Paulie joined Marcia Manning in a stream of high-pitched curses.

Jake grabbed E.D.'s and Destiny's hands, and the three of them bolted for the schoolroom. They slammed the door behind them and sank onto the floor with laughter.

Chapter Twenty-nine

The day of the opening was going to go down in her personal history as the longest, most exhausting, most difficult day of her entire life, E.D. thought. Maybe someday she'd write about it.

That morning there had been costumes that still needed hemming, stage lights that needed refocusing. The meadow, where the actors had been parking ever since they started rehearsing at Wit's End, needed to be mowed and signs put up to let the audience know it was the parking lot. Hal and Cordelia hadn't finished painting the set. The phone kept ringing with questions and ticket orders. Besides fixing the regular meals, Govindaswami had decided to bake cookies and make punch to sell at intermission, so he needed more help than usual. A number of cast members took the day off work, and the high school kids on the tech crews skipped school to come help. E.D.'s friend Melissa skipped school, too, and came to do whatever she could. E.D. didn't have any time to spend with her, though. She had rushed from one task to another all day, trying to keep track of everything and everybody.

Her father was the only one who wasn't worried about the weather. He claimed that the theater gods were on their side and that the clouds that kept darkening the sky and threatening storms would blow over before the audience was due to arrive. And always, everywhere, Marcia Manning and the television crew were in the way, aiming cameras and shoving microphones in people's faces and tripping people with their electrical cables.

Somehow, though, by the time cars started arriving and Jeremy was sent out to direct them to parking places, almost everything was ready. Even the problem of Destiny's ears had been solved. Lucille had made him a hat, which he wore in every scene, even when he was dressed in pajamas. A line had been added about Hans loving hats.

No one had remembered to give E.D. a count of the

opening night tickets that had been given away, so more people were showing up than there were seats. Extra folding chairs had to be squeezed in, and family members of the cast were sent up to the loft with the sound and lighting technicians.

As curtain time approached, E.D. looked out at the barn full of people from the stage manager's station offstage left, and realized that through all the rehearsals and barn renovation, she had never quite believed it would happen, that there would really be a Wit's End Playhouse that real live people would come to. Yet there they were, a hundred and seventy-seven of them, Jake's grandfather next to Marcia Manning and the producer in the front row, and three cameramen stationed in the aisles.

She took a deep breath and gave the signal for the houselights to go down. Jeremy Bernstein began to play the overture on his accordion, miked so that speakers carried the music to the farthest corners of the barn. During the overture, the nuns had to come past E.D. one at a time so that she could light their candles. Randolph had decided to begin the show with a candlelight procession, the candles the nuns carried as they chanted their way around the stage providing the only light. That way they didn't need to build a separate set for the abbey chapel.

E.D.'s hands shook as she held the lighter to the wick of one candle after another. This must be what stage fright feels like, she thought. Her stomach was tied in knots. She didn't think stage managers were supposed to get stage fright. The overture ended, and the note was given for the chant to begin. *"Dixit Dominus Domino meo,"* the soloist sang as she stepped out onto the stage with her candle, and the show began.

There were thirteen scenes in the first act. By the time the fifth scene, where Maria taught the von Trapp children to sing "Do-Re-Mi," was over, E.D.'s stage fright had disappeared. None of the awful things she had imagined, none of the glitches from dress rehearsal, had happened so far. The actors had all remembered their lines and the words to their songs. Jeremy was playing the right songs at the right time. The lights were coming up and going down when she gave the cue. All the children were doing exactly what they were supposed to do. Even Destiny. And the audience was applauding when they were supposed to. Maybe her father was right. Maybe the theater gods were on their side!

And so it seemed, right through the rest of the first act, through intermission (the audience talked and laughed and seemed to be enjoying themselves, and Govindaswami sold out all his cookies and punch), and on into the second act.

Until the next to the last scene—at the Kaltzburg Festival Concert. The scene began with Captain von

Trapp playing the guitar and singing the eidelweiss song, with Maria and the seven von Trapp children gathered around him. Distant thunder began to make itself heard beneath the music. Then, during the last two lines of the song, rain began to patter on the barn roof. As the song ended and the audience began to applaud, the sound of the rain on the roof grew in intensity. When the actor came on to announce that the Nazi escort had arrived to take Captain von Trapp to his command in the German navy, rain dripped off his nose as he began to speak.

Throughout his speech the rain drummed harder and he spoke louder, until, by the end, he was shouting at the top of his lungs to be heard introducing the von Trapps' encore song. Thunder drowned out the first notes of the accordion. Captain von Trapp, Maria, and the seven children lined up to sing, all of them looking intently toward where Jeremy was playing the introduction to the song. E.D. couldn't hear the music over the pounding of the rain, and it was clear that none of the actors could, either.

"Bring the musician's sound up!" E.D. whispered into her microphone to the sound technician. "The actors can't hear!"

She had to strain to make out the reply through her headphones. "I did already. It's up full!"

The actors were standing onstage now in position, their hands clasped in front of them as they should be.

But they didn't begin to sing. Nine pairs of eyes focused desperately on Jeremy, who was clearly playing music that could not be heard. Thunder crashed again. Suddenly the actor who had announced the song appeared onstage again, holding a large microphone. He spoke directly into it, and the sound rose just slightly above the level of the rain on the roof.

"Ladies and gentlemen, the Kaltzburg Festival Concert will continue in a moment, when the storm passes over the mountains. In the meantime, let us all sing together the song the von Trapps sang earlier—'Do-Re-Mi.' I'm sure you all know it! Please join us!"

He sang the first line loudly into the microphone, and the actors onstage joined him. Soon the whole audience was singing along, and E.D. realized the great advantage of doing a show that almost everyone already knew.

After two rousing repetitions of "Do-Re-Mi" sung into and over the rain and thunder, the pounding on the roof began to slack off. As the song reached its conclusion the third time around, Captain von Trapp stepped forward and took the microphone from the other actor, who had stayed onstage, conducting the audience. He held up one hand for silence and began the last notes of the song, his voice going down and down to a deep bass. "Do ti la so fa me re . . ." He paused, looking out at the audience, and then signaled for the last "do."

The audience shouted "Do!" and then leaped to their feet, cheering and stamping and applauding. Captain von Trapp waited till they had settled down and taken their seats again and then waved to Jeremy to begin their encore song.

E.D. breathed a sigh of relief as the song went perfectly, each pair of children singing their farewell and leaving the stage until only Destiny was left, standing between Maria and Captain von Trapp. When he sang that the sun had gone to bed, with the rain still pattering gently overhead, the audience laughed. "I'll say!" someone called out. Destiny, undaunted, finished his line, sang his good-bye, and exited. The applause when the song ended was as loud and enthusiastic as before. The rest of the scene, as the Germans discover that the von Trapps have fled, went perfectly. E.D. was just about to call for the stage lights to go out when outside there was a blue-white flash so bright that it could be seen through every crack in the barn siding, followed instantly by what sounded like an explosion. The lights went out and E.D.'s earphones went dead.

"Can anybody hear me?" E.D. whispered into her microphone. Nothing. Even the tiny light over her prompt book had gone out, and it was pitch-black backstage. "Electricity's out!" she said in a stage whisper. "Set up for the final scene, and I'll think of something. Somebody tell Jeremy to keep playing until somebody comes to tell him to stop." She hoped he could play without being able to see the music.

E.D. went over the end of the show in her mind. Even with lights, the final scene was fairly dark. It took place outdoors at night in the abbey's garden, with the von Trapps hiding while the Nazis searched the abbey to find them. When Jake's character, Rolf, came onstage, it was his flashlight that allowed him to see Captain von Trapp and Maria. The lights were supposed to come up enough that the audience could see them before Rolf did. Then, when Rolf had already called out to his lieutenant, he had to see Liesl, again in the light from his flashlight, and decide not to turn the family over to the Nazis.

Without any stage lights the audience would be able to see whoever Jake, as Rolf, lit with his flashlight, but they wouldn't be able to see that it was Rolf *holding* the flashlight. They wouldn't understand that it was Rolf's love for Liesl that kept him from turning them all in, that led him to call out to his lieutenant that there was no one in the garden. Without *some* light on the stage, so that the audience could see the moment of suspense as Rolf decides what to do, the ending wouldn't make sense. How could they get enough light onstage to make it work?

Nuns! Nuns with candles. The scene was the abbey, and the nuns were supposed to come on at the very end for the final song anyway. There could be as many nuns onstage as they needed. The actors who played the nuns in the first act would already be back in their habits, ready for the end of the show. All E.D. needed to do was gather them up before the scene began and get their candles lit again. They could stand in a semicircle around the abbey garden, and their candles would almost certainly give enough light for the audience to know what was going on. The stage crew was busy setting up for the final scene, working in the light from Jake's flashlight. "Jake!"

"What? What are we going to do?"

"We need all the nuns, right away. With their candles." Quickly, she outlined her plan, and he grunted agreement. "And get another candle or two for Jeremy so he can play the last song." She took the flashlight and kept it trained so that the crew could finish changing the scene, while Jake went to tell the other actors what they needed to do.

This time as the nuns gathered and she lit their candles, her hand was perfectly steady. It would work. She knew it. Already she could see in her mind's eye the scene as the Mother Abbess began singing the final reprise of "Climb Ev'ry Mountain," the other nuns joining in and lighting the way for the von Trapps to begin their climb over the Austrian Alps into Switzerland and freedom. She felt almost as excited as if she were helping the real family escape from the Nazis.

Chapter Thirty

aves, every last one of them!" Randolph said. It wasn't news anymore, Jake thought. The family—including Hal—had gathered in the living room with pitchers of Govindaswami's now-famous Playhouse Punch and platters of cookies to read the reviews together. Everyone had already read and reread them, probably memorizing, as he had, the parts about them.

Randolph waved the local paper. "The *Gazette* says Traybridge has never seen such a level of professionalism and talent from a local cast." He read from the page in his hand. "Worthy of Broadway, he calls it. Well—he's probably never actually seen a Broadway production. Still, listen to this: 'The board of the Traybridge Little Theatre needs to ask itself why it canceled such a stellar production. If the new Wit's End Playhouse chooses to mount a whole season, our local theater isn't likely to survive the competition.' Take that, Mrs. Montrose!"

"You are not, of course, considering a whole season," Sybil said. "You wouldn't—"

"Couldn't," Zedediah said. "There's no heat in the barn."

"What about summer?" Hal asked. "We could do shows in the summer!" The reviews had all mentioned the original, ingenious, beautifully painted sets, and Hal had apparently rethought his mission in life. The sign on his bedroom door now read HAL APPLEWHITE, SCULPTOR AND SET DESIGNER.

Archie shook his head. "No air-conditioning either."

"We *could* do two productions a year," Randolph said. "One in the fall and one in the spring. I'm considering the possibility."

Sybil groaned. "I'll have to start turning out Petunia Grantham mysteries by the dozen to raise the money, then. Do you have any idea how much this production cost?"

Randolph waved his hand dismissively. "You can't

count the cost of renovating the barn—a few productions as successful as this one and we're bound to make that up. Besides, you had ground to a halt on the Great American Novel anyway and you know it. No point pretending. Petunia Grantham is in your blood."

"If we do another musical," Cordelia said, "there needs to be a lot more dancing."

"No nuns!" This was Lucille. "I will never make another habit as long as I live."

"You wouldn't need to," Sybil said. "We own twenty of them now."

"Listen to this," Bernstein said, holding up a printout from the Internet. "It's from Charlotte. 'The intriguing choice to use an accordion rather than an orchestra gave the production an air of Tyrolean folk authenticity that was entirely new. The accordion's ability to mimic the sound of an organ was a bonus for the abbey scenes.'"

"My favorite," Lucille said, "is the one from Raleigh. 'Rainbow Cast Antidote to Third Reich's Racism' is the headline. The reviewer says, 'After the initial surprise of seeing an African American playing Maria, the audience lost all awareness of skin color—an important lesson for us all.'"

"What did I tell you!" Randolph said.

"That's the one that talks about the candles, isn't it?" E.D. asked.

Lucille nodded and read on. "'The use of candles to

light the last scene set the final rendition of "Climb Ev'ry Mountain" apart and provided a powerful metaphor. The von Trapp Family Singers throughout their musical career lit candles rather than cursing the dark.' "

"Good thing I had the foresight to do the candlelight procession at the top of the show," Randolph said. "It isn't in the script, you know."

E.D. bristled. "Don't you dare take credit for my idea! Quick thinking under pressure, that's what *that* was."

"All right, all right. But I had the good sense to decide to keep it in."

Jake was only half listening. His part was so small he hadn't expected to find himself mentioned in the reviews. But to his astonishment he'd been in almost all of them. He'd made copies to send to his parents. "Mature performance from a promising teen in a small but pivotal role," one of them said. "Convincing both as adolescent suitor and Nazi," another reviewer wrote. "With commanding stage presence, Jake Semple turned in a performance equal to any in this impressive production. We expect to hear more from this young man with the mellifluous singing voice." Jake had looked up "mellifluous." *Flowing with honey or sweetness.* Never had anyone mentioned sweetness and Jake Semple in the same sentence before. He would send a copy to his social worker in Rhode Island.

"Read the one about me," Destiny said. He was lying on the floor next to Winston, drawing with fluorescent markers.

"The youngest von Trapp, transformed from a girl named Gretl to a hat-obsessed little boy named Hans, was played with uncommon gusto by Destiny Applewhite."

"Uncommon gusto," Sybil repeated. "That's you, all right."

That, Jake thought, was the whole Applewhite clan. Govindaswami and Bernstein, too.

A butterfly fluttered in and landed on Govindaswami's shoulder. Govindaswami raised his glass of punch, and the butterfly stepped delicately onto the edge and unrolled its tongue to drink.

Paulie, who had stayed on in the main house after the television crew left, raised his wings, gave a couple of small hops along his perch, and swore.

"That's a new one," Zedediah said.

"He learned it from Marcia Manning," Cordelia said.

It was the only lasting thing the television people had left behind, Jake thought. The lightning bolt that knocked out the power had struck their satellite dish, and they'd gathered up their roasted equipment and left the morning after the opening. The next day Bernstein had gotten an e-mail message from the network explaining that the producer had gone off to a spa to recuperate from nervous exhaustion and Ms. Manning had taken a job with a competing network. Consequently, the Applewhite spot, originally planned for twelve minutes of prime time, would be cut to two and a half. It might air, they said, on a slow news day as the human interest piece at the end of the evening news.

Bernstein had taken the news pretty well. "Associate producer doesn't mean much of anything anyway." He had managed to sell an article on the way television's mass-market focus cheapened art to the journal that had originally given him the Sybil Jameson assignment.

Now that *The Sound of Music* was up and running and would be over within another week, Jake thought, the Applewhites would be getting back to normal. Whatever that was. Jeremy was planning to stay on to work on his book about the family. Govindaswami was going to an ashram in Idaho to lecture on cooking as meditation. Randolph had gotten a call from a theater in Pennsylvania to do a "rainbow" *Sound of Music* as their Christmas show. E.D. was already revising her curriculum plan. She was planning a project on goat husbandry to take the place of the completed butterfly project.

As for Jake, the only thing he knew for certain was that somehow or another he was going to get himself on the stage again. He had an answer now to

Zedediah's question about what gave him joy. He wasn't about to waste a mellifluous voice and commanding stage presence.

An adventurous quest for the meaning of life, involving the ability to think things through. The banner was back up in the schoolroom where the barn renovation schedule had been. Jake didn't know any more about the meaning of life than he had the first day he came to Wit's End. But whatever else he could say about the way the Applewhites lived, it certainly was an adventurous quest. And he was beginning to get some idea of the value of thinking things through.

Winston, pointedly ignoring Govindaswami's butterfly, sighed and rolled over, his head coming to rest on Jake's foot. Jake scratched behind his ears. Destiny was humming as he drew. He looked up at Jake. "What color are you going to make your hair when the show is over?" he asked.

"I don't know," Jake said. "What color do you think?"

"Blond," Destiny said. "Like mine."

Jake shrugged. "I think maybe brown. Like mine."

The outrageous Applewhite family returns in
Stephanie S. Tolan's new novel

APPLEWHITES AT WIT'S END

Chapter One

It was a dark and stormy night when Randolph Applewhite arrived home from New York to announce the end of the world. The whole family plus Jake Semple, the extra student at their home school, the Creative Academy, were gathered at the time around the fireplace in the living room of the main house at Wit's End, while a wind howled and snow swirled against the windows.

Like everyone else, E.D. had at first taken her father's announcement to be hyperbole—one of her vocabulary words for that week, which meant "deliberate and obvious exaggeration for effect." A famous theater director, Randolph Applewhite had a habit of making exactly this announcement whenever something—almost anything—went wrong with a project of his and he felt the need for sympathy. So often had they heard it, in fact, that E.D.'s mother, the even more famous Sybil Jameson, author of the bestselling Petunia Grantham mystery novels, actually said, "That's nice, dear," as she struggled to pick up a stitch she had dropped in the scarf she was attempting to knit.

It wasn't until well into his explanation that she put down her needles and began paying attention. "What do you mean gone?"

"Just what I said! Gone! Embezzled!"

"How much of it?"

"All of it! To the last penny. The Applewhite family is destitute. We shall have to sell Wit's End and move to a hovel somewhere."

"What's a hovel?" asked E.D.'s five-year-old brother, Destiny, who was cheerfully and industriously drawing a bright spring-green pig on a large pad of newsprint.

When the whole story had at last been told—not until long after Destiny had been sent to bed and everyone else had finished a couple of mugs of hot cocoa enhanced with comforting marshmallows or alcohol, depending on their ages—it was clear that while the end of the Applewhites' world had not yet arrived, it was looming on the horizon like smoke from a wildfire and heading their way.

E.D. had never really understood—nor felt the need to—the financial structure that formed the foundation of her family's creative compound. She only knew that the whole, extended Applewhite family had left New York when Destiny was a year old and moved to rural North Carolina, where they had bought an abandoned motor lodge called the Bide-A-Wee. They had renamed it Wit's End and had lived here since, the adults following their particular creative passions and the children, except for E.D.'s own absolutely noncreative self, *discovering* theirs. All of the adults were famous. Her grandfather and her uncle Archie both designed and created furniture—Zedediah Applewhite's handcrafted wood furniture and Archie's "Furniture of the Absurd," which wasn't really so much furniture as sculpture and which was regularly exhibited in galleries around the country. Her aunt Lucille was a poet.

What E.D. learned that stormy winter night was that they had come to Wit's End not just so the family could live together, but so that they could pool their resources in order to continue their work. The vast majority of these resources came from the worldwide sales of the Petunia Grantham mysteries; some came from Zedediah's beautiful, expensive, and entirely practical furniture; and some came from Randolph's work directing plays. Nothing else anyone did brought in much money. All of their resources had been gathered together in a family trust. The manager who had handled that trust, and therefore the future of the entire Applewhite enterprise, had turned out to be a crook.

"He'll go to jail," Randolph said after his second cup of bourbon-laced cocoa. "There's that, at least!"

"And what good will that do *us*?" Archie asked.

"I, for one, will feel better," Randolph answered. "It will cheer the dark nights in our hovel."

Zedediah, ever practical, pointed out that the Petunia Grantham mysteries would no doubt continue to sell as they always had, to which Sybil responded that she had only that morning killed Petunia Grantham off. The current novel, which was due to be finished within the week, would be the last in the series. "I killed her because I simply can't write another one. It would destroy my very soul."

"Your soul is tougher than that!" Randolph responded. "You can simply resurrect her in the next! They do it all the time in soap operas."

"My books are not soap operas!"

Only Aunt Lucille had taken the news of their sudden poverty in stride. She breathed a series of long, calming breaths, smiled, and announced that they would get along in some unforeseen way, just as they always had. All they needed to do was trust their creative energies, and they would surely come up with a way to solve the problem. "One step at a time," she said. "Out of the darkness, into the light."

"How long do we have?" Sybil asked then.

"If we gather up everything we have in the bank accounts, plus whatever you're owed when you turn in the current novel, plus the fees for the two directing gigs I have contracts for—assuming that Zedediah's furniture continues to sell the way it has—we can probably keep the mortgage paid through June. Maybe July. But after that . . ."

"We'll think of something," Lucille said. "Remember Shelley's 'Ode to the West Wind.' *'O Wind, / If Winter comes, can Spring be far behind?'*"

As it turned out, the winter was unusually harsh and unusually long, or at least it felt that way. By the time the Wit's End daffodils began blooming in March, the family had become obsessed with saving money in every way possible. The children's allowances had been not just cut, but actually discontinued. E.D.'s older brother, Hal, unable now to order sculpture supplies online for UPS delivery, had taken to going through the trash to find materials for his projects. "If it gets much worse," he complained, "I'll have to go back to painting! At least I have plenty of tubes of paint."

E.D.'s sister, Cordelia, had given up drinking her seaweed-and-protein health drinks. "I can't even afford the gas to get to the store, let alone the cost of the supplements! How am I going to maintain the energy to keep up my dancing?"

Winston, their food-loving basset hound, was now living on kibble instead of canned dog food, and liver treats had become a thing of the past. Zedediah's parrot, Paulie, could no longer count on fresh peanuts, and meat had become an occasional indulgence instead of the centerpiece of most dinners for the humans in the family. Pot roast, everybody's favorite dinner, had not been seen since the end of the world was announced. E.D. thought she had seen Uncle Archie at the goat pen from time to time, staring longingly at Wolfbane and Witch Hazel, Lucille's rescue goats.

E.D. herself had begun using the back sides of papers from the recycling box to write her research papers for school. And Zedediah had sped up production of his furniture, appearing in the kitchen late for dinner, still wearing his sawdust-covered work apron, and going right back to the woodshop afterward. So busy was he that Paulie had begun picking his feathers out from loneliness and perches had to be established for him throughout Wit's End. The last person to leave a room was supposed to take Paulie along so that he wouldn't be left by himself.

It was an evening in early March when Randolph, having just been paid by the theater in Raleigh where he'd directed a production of the musical *Oliver!* with

Jake, his newly discovered star, playing the role of the Artful Dodger, called a family meeting. He waved his check in the air. "This will cover another mortgage payment," he said. The Applewhites couldn't always be counted upon to celebrate one another's successes, but this time they broke into spontaneous cheers and applause. "Even better, I have a plan to save Wit's End!"

The cheers and applause died away. No one entirely trusted Randolph's ideas. "What is it?" E.D.'s mother asked suspiciously. She had steadfastly refused—citing the arrival of her Petunia Grantham royalty check as her fair contribution to the family bank account—to resurrect Petunia or begin another book, as she felt the need to rest her brain. "Your plans have been known to require considerable effort from the rest of us."

"All for one and one for all," Randolph said. "Just listen to me, everyone. You're going to love it!" He turned to Jake, who was sitting on the floor rubbing Winston's ears. "I owe a part of this idea to Jake. I was sitting in the theater, listening to him sing 'Consider Yourself at Home,' when it came to me. The next line of the song invites Oliver Twist into the family, just as we've invited Jake into ours. So there I was, looking at this stage full of singing and dancing kids—Fagin's pickpockets—and it occurred to me that we could create just such a family."

"A family of pickpockets?" Archie said. "I hardly

think that's the best way to solve our problem!"

"A family of creative kids! We invited Jake to join the Creative Academy. Why couldn't we take in a whole lot more? Not all year round—just in the summer. We'll start a camp for creative kids. I've even got a name for it. *Eureka!*" Randolph looked expectantly around the room. "Well? What do you think? People pay big money to send their kids to summer camp. Just regular summer camp. Think what they'd pay to have their kids spend eight weeks with a family of professional artists. *Famous professional artists*!"

"Kids? Living here with us?" Hal said, his face going pale. "How many?"

"I'm thinking just twelve this first year, a pilot group."

"And what would we do with these twelve kids?" Archie asked.

"Teach them. Encourage them. Share with them our love of art, our own individual creative passions. Set them on the path to becoming creative, productive adults! *Eureka!* would not only bring in big bucks, it would be a humanitarian endeavor—helping to groom the next generation of American artists. It will be a whole family project. There will be something for everyone to do."

"Me, too?" asked Destiny.

"Of course you, too. You can be the camp mascot!"

E.D. doubted that Destiny knew what a mascot was, but the title was enough to satisfy him.

Randolph turned to his wife. "Now that Petunia Grantham's dead, you're going to need something to do! You can't rest your brain forever!"

"Twelve children? Twelve *other people's* children?"

"Yes. Think of it. Twelve delightful children into whose meager little lives we will bring the joys of art. We do art—and children—uncommonly well. Just look at our own four, and Jake, too, of course! Who would have thought when Jake first came to us that we could turn him into a musical-theater star in a matter of weeks? We could do that sort of thing with twelve more!"

E.D. suspected that Jake wasn't willing to give the Applewhite family *all* the credit for his newly discovered talent, but she could see that he was listening carefully as Randolph laid out the details of the camp. Each of them would share with the campers what they liked to do best, Randolph told them—their own creative passion—including Jake. As the only one besides Destiny able to sing at all, he could be the singing coach.

"And what would *I* share with them?" E.D. asked.

"A play needs a stage manager, a camp needs a—a—*an executive assistant*, the person who handles the schedule and the details and makes sure everything runs smoothly. You do that wonderfully well, E.D—you know you do!"

No one but Destiny had yet accepted the idea. So Randolph went on, refusing to be daunted by their stony faces. "For heaven's sake, people. We're talking only eight weeks here! Practically no time at all. If we charge twelve families what I expect to charge them, we could save Wit's End, bring meat back to the family table, and restart allowances. Would you really rather sell out, leave here, and move to a hovel in Hoboken?"

Chapter Two

When Jake had first come to live at Wit's End, he had been determined to get away as soon as possible. Having been kicked out of the entire public school system of the state of Rhode Island, then out of Traybridge Middle School after he was sent to North Carolina to live with his grandfather, he had expected to get himself kicked out of the Applewhites' Creative Academy in a matter of days. The first problem with that had been that the Applewhites weren't the least bit bothered by his multiple piercings, his scarlet spiked hair, his black clothes, or his cursing—all the things that established his identity as the bad kid from the city. The second problem was that he really had no place else to go. His parents were both serving time in minimum-security prisons for having attempted to sell their homegrown marijuana to an off-duty sheriff's deputy, and there were no foster families back home in Providence willing to take him in. E.D. had almost gleefully pointed out that his only alternative was Juvie. So he'd been forced to stay.

It had turned out to be the best thing that ever happened to him. Becoming a musical-theater star in a matter of weeks had surprised Jake as much as it had surprised the Applewhites. He'd never suspected that he had a talent for singing and acting until Randolph recruited him to play Rolf in *The Sound of Music*. The show had been a success and Jake had gotten good reviews, but that hadn't been nearly as important as his discovery of what the Applewhites called a "creative passion." Never in his life had Jake been anywhere near as happy as he was onstage, in front of an audience, becoming a person quite different from himself. He loved singing. He loved acting. And later when Randolph cast him as the Artful Dodger in *Oliver!*, he'd found out that he loved dancing, too. Everything about musical theater, in fact, turned Jake on.

Because the Creative Academy was a home school, he had been able to take off the whole month of February to be in *Oliver!*; and not only that, he'd been able to get school credit for doing it. He was theoretically in the seventh grade with E.D., but he didn't have to be stuck all the time doing what she did and being shown up by her obsessively organized, determinedly academic, and viciously competitive version of education. This was a girl who drove herself relentlessly toward perfection and couldn't bear the thought of getting (actually, thanks to the way the Applewhites did home schooling, *giving herself*) less than an A in anything. She and Jake might be very nearly the same age, but they were wildly and impossibly different. Thanks to the Applewhite philosophy of life, which passionately celebrated individuality, that was completely okay.

Randolph's end-of-the-world announcement had scared Jake clear down to his toes, though he'd done his best to hide it. What would suddenly poverty-stricken Applewhites do with *him*? He himself had no money. His grandfather was providing him with a small allowance so he could pay for clothes and a few incidentals, but otherwise he'd really been taken in as if he were a family member. He wasn't. He was another mouth to feed. Jake couldn't stand to lose his place here—it would mean losing himself. His new self. The only one he'd ever really known or cared about!

The morning after that dark and stormy night he'd worked up the nerve to ask Archie and Lucille—it was their Wisteria Cottage that he lived in—if they thought it was going to be possible for him to finish the school year.

"Don't be silly, Jake!" Lucille had proclaimed, "You're a full-time student. Of *course* you'll finish the year."

But as time went on and the austerity measures the Applewhites had adopted began to really pinch, Jake had started worrying about what would happen in the summer. Like regular schools, the Creative Academy's year ended in June. There'd be no reason to keep him here after that, so he figured they would probably send him to the grandfather he barely knew, a grandfather who had no clue about creative passion and who had only seen one musical in all his life: *The Sound of Music* last October at Wit's End Playhouse.

So when Randolph announced his idea for *Eureka!*, Jake had mostly held his breath until he heard the words he'd been hoping for: that he was to have a job to do at the camp. He didn't care that he didn't have the first clue about how to be a singing coach. He only cared that he wasn't going to be sent off to spend the summer alone on a ramshackle farm outside of Traybridge with his grandfather. Whatever camp turned out to be, it had to be better than that! He figured he was the happiest person in the room when the rest of the family had finally agreed to it.

CHAPTER TWO CONTINUES...